I0698916

# BLUE-SKINNED MYSTICS

## A LITERARY FANTASY TALE

ANITHA KRISHNAN

DREAM PEDLAR BOOKS

Copyright © 2025 by Anitha Krishnan

All rights reserved.

No part of this book may be reproduced in any form or by any electronic or mechanical means, including information storage and retrieval systems, without written permission from the author, except for the use of brief quotations in a book review.

This book is a work of fiction. Names, characters, places and incidents are either the product of the author's imagination or are used fictitiously, and any resemblance to actual persons, living or dead, locales, or events is entirely coincidental.

Ebook ISBN: 978-1-998472-15-4

Paperback ISBN: 978-1-998472-16-1

Cover stock image: 'Mystic woman face with floral ornament. Drawing on paper, Color effect. Eye contact. Computer collage. — Illustration' by @JozefKlopacka on Depositphotos; Standard License purchased on 15 March 2021

❀ Formatted with Vellum

*For the mystic that resides in each one of us,*
*We already possess the wisdom we seek.*

~

*For Abhinav & Dhruv,*
*The greatest miracles in my life. Love, always.*

~

# ABOUT THIS BOOK

### Blue-Skinned Mystics

*Magic saved his village. Now, magic wants his soul.*

The blue-skinned mystics descend on the village of Hanish, a land ravaged by drought and famine, and transform it into an oasis.

All it takes to heal the barren village is a single drop of tear that rolls down the cheek of eight-year-old Ari.

Or so it seems, until Ari begins to turn blue. Evidently, the saviours of his land intend to take more than they have given.

Sacrifices must be made for the greater good. And an innocent drop of tear is not enough.

*Blue-Skinned Mystics* is a literary fantasy tale, a coming-of-age story steeped in magic and mysticism, and a reminder that growing up entails its fair share of loss — of innocence, of simple-minded faith, and of the uncomplicated wonders of childhood.

# CHAPTER 1

# THE ARRIVAL OF THE MYSTICS

Ari and Jana gawked unabashedly as the first of the caravans trundled into their village. Painted in the colours of spring, the wagons appeared like a moving meadow in the distance. A floating patch of green dotted with the reds and yellows of new blooms.

A splash of colour in the dreary land of Hanish, where the earth had turned barren and the wells had run dry two summers ago, where the last of their old and the weak had died a summer ago, and where the first child had given up her ghost three days ago. The granddaughter of the village chief, who had, until then, held out against repeated calls to seek the aid of the blue-skinned mystics.

The caravans now came closer. A reminder of what Hanish had once been, of what it had lost. Like a promise of all that it could be again. Fertile. Prosperous.

The wheels hardly kicked up dust for they barely touched the ground. Even the horses pulling the caravans trotted in mid-air, although only a fraction of an inch above the ground.

An anomaly that only the most astute of observers could discern.

Ari looked up at his father to see if he too had noticed how the horses and the caravans were moving in mid-air. But his father's gaze was directed firmly at the windows of the caravans, his eyes scanning and searching, eager for a glimpse of the blue-skinned mystics who had come to save his land and his people.

"The caravans are floating," Jana whispered into Ari's ear. Her words smelled of the last slice of bread she and Ari had shared that morning.

*The last breakfast*, mother had warned them, when Jana had started to whine about how stale the bread appeared and how foul it tasted. Upon hearing their mother's words, the siblings had quickly wolfed down their share of the slice without further complaint.

"I know," Ari whispered back.

"But how?"

Ari shrugged. "Magic?"

Jana snorted. "Magic does not explain everything."

"That's how the mystics are going to heal our land."

"But—ow!" Jana's retort was cut short as a sharp rap landed on her head. Ari yelped as two fingers twisted and pulled at his ear.

"Quiet, you two!" their father hissed, letting go of Ari's ear.

Tears of pain stung Ari's eyes, but he was determined to not shed them. He was all of eight years old. A big boy now. Almost a young man, as his parents reminded him every so often, especially when they needed him to fetch water from the neighbouring village, three miles away. It was a chore he despised on days when there was no food in his belly and his mouth was so dry his tongue stuck to the roof.

But Jana, five years older than he was, had it worse. She had to carry their baby brother, Nayo, everywhere in a sling on her back, occasionally placing a wet rag in his mouth for him to chew on, while their mother and father along with every other adult in the village worked at the step-well all day. Digging and excavating, praying that the earth would give up a few more drops of water to parch their thirsty throats.

Despite his efforts, tears filled Ari's eyes and blurred his vision. And so he didn't see the blue-skinned lad who had approached him and now stood in front of him.

Ari's father placed a protective hand on his boy's shoulder.

Ari blinked. A tear spilled over his eye and rolled down his cheek and off his jaw.

The blue boy caught the falling tear in the palm of his hand. He brought his cupped hand to his face and blew gently on it. He then bent and smeared the tear on the cracked and weathered ground right in front of where Ari stood, mesmerized, his tears frozen and forgotten in surprise.

The blue boy then stepped back a few paces, not once shifting his gaze from the ground he had rubbed with his hand.

Ari glanced at the boy, then at the ground in front of him, expecting something to happen.

And it did.

A tiny sprig pushed its way out of the ground. Gasps filled the air around him.

Ari looked up and saw the villagers had crowded around them. His father's hand on his shoulder was heavy, his grip tight, as if it was the adult man who needed to lean on his little boy for support.

Under the watchful eyes of the villagers, the sprig grew, whirling and twirling and unfurling in a dance. Its stem grew longer and thicker. Leaves and branches and more leaves bloomed from its central stalk, which pushed skywards, reaching for something unknown, something unseen, in the vast blue far above them all.

Ari and the villagers stepped back to allow room for the plant, now a young tree, to grow. Its trunk grew thicker and wider, and Ari estimated it would take him and Jana and three of their friends to be able to form a ring around it, clasping each other's hands. Its roots travelled through the ground under their feet, until it reached the edges of their village.

The blue boy was now out of sight, hidden behind the wide trunk of this strange tree he had coaxed out of the barren earth of Hanish, and now that it had sprung into existence, it simply couldn't stop growing.

The tree spread its branches all around, casting an unfamiliar cool shade over everyone touched by its shadow.

Small white flowers blossomed on the tree. Their scent was unfamiliar, heady and intoxicating. A whiff of musk. The briefest trace of rose. Lavender, perhaps. Not quite any of them. But an enticing concoction of several fragrances, very few known, most of them unfamiliar, enveloped everyone who stood there.

And then the fruits burst forth. They were a strange blue, almost indigo in colour, and each was shaped like a teardrop.

As everyone watched the miracles unfolding on the high branches, Ari and Jana slipped along the inner edge of the circle the villagers had formed around the tree until they could see the blue boy again.

The blue boy brought his hands together in a gesture of worship, whispered something like a prayer and bowed to the tree.

He then tugged at the fruit hanging closest to him. The tree sighed, reluctant to part with its fruit. Its leaves rustled in annoyance even though there was no wind. The blue boy let go of the fruit, and the branch pulled itself back and out of reach.

The boy looked up at the tree, his face a question. For a few moments, he gazed at the tree, which had grown so tall and wide Ari couldn't see where its highest branches were.

And then the blue boy looked straight at Ari. He held out a hand.

Ari looked at him. At this stranger in their midst. He looked like one of those older kids in Hanish, the ones who could go wherever they pleased, whenever they desired, and do whatever they wanted, even if most of the time they tended to keep looking over their shoulders to ensure there were no witnesses to their misdeeds.

They were only looking for admonishing grown-ups, Ari had realized long back, for they never seemed to spot Ari on the few occasions he managed to sneak up on them.

This was all in the days before the drought and the famine. Now all those mischief-makers had been recruited alongside all the adults to dig to the centre of the earth in search of water, and it was the little ones like Ari and the other small boys in the village, the seven- and eight- and nine- and ten-year-olds who could roam the streets as they trekked three miles to the next village and three miles back for a pailful of water. With no one to watch over them, they had all the time and freedom to play truant like the older kids used to. Only, it turned out they no longer had the desire to.

But now, looking at the blue boy, extending a hand to him like an invitation into a secret world, Ari was reminded of all the times he had wanted to turn sixteen years old overnight just so he could blow clouds of smoke, drink secret fluids hidden in opaque flasks, and kiss girls on their lips in a way that made them blush.

And without a second thought, he stepped forward and placed his hand in the blue boy's.

"Ari!" His father's voice sounded like a whiplash on his back. His father had perhaps only just realized his hand was no longer on Ari's shoulder but hung limply by his side.

"Ari, come back," his father shouted.

But Ari did not stop. He did not look back. He didn't even flinch.

The blue boy smiled at Ari, as if pleased with his commitment. Ari smiled back, a little pleased with himself at the test he had passed.

The blue boy held Ari's hand gently. Ari wondered if the colour had been merely painted on and whether some of it would rub off on him.

But Ari had no time to find out as the boy, still holding Ari's hand in his, pointed up towards the tree. Ari looked up.

The tree stooped towards Ari and bent a branch so low a bunch of the strange blue fruits hung right in front of him. The blue boy pointed at the fruit and then at Ari.

Ari wondered if the boy was mute or whether he had simply chosen to not disturb the events unravelling around them with speech.

Ari let go of the boy's hand, then reached out to grab a fruit with both hands. He waited for a moment, half-expecting the tree to sigh and pull the fruit-laden branch away and out of reach.

When it didn't, Ari gently twisted the fruit, the way his father had taught him to when the apple orchards in the village had been in full bloom three years ago. The tree released the fruit instantly. It felt warm and soft in his hands.

Ari looked at the blue boy, who produced a small knife concealed within his blue robes. Ari took the knife and sliced the fruit.

The thin outer peel yielded easily to the pressure of the knife. Inside, the fruit was a soft but firm pulp that clung to the peel. Not crunchy like an apple. Not fleshy like slices of an orange. This was something different altogether.

Ari offered the first slice to the blue boy. The boy was pleased with this gesture. A huge grin broke on his face, his teeth unnaturally white against the dark blue of his lips and face. Like a full moon shining eerily against the blue-black of the night.

The boy shook his head and pointed back towards Ari. Ari bit into the first slice. Juicy sweetness exploded in his mouth as he chewed on the pulp. The morsel trickled down his throat, cooling him like a drink from the freshwater spring that used to gurgle through Hanish a long time ago.

Elated, Ari cut another slice and ran towards Jana, eager to share this new discovery with her. Jana's eyes lit up as she bit into the slice Ari offered her.

Ari's father was the next to partake of the strange fruit. Tears of joy sprung to his eyes as the juicy sweetness of the pulp soothed his dry mouth and pampered it with a taste and fragrance he had long forgotten even existed in the world.

He went up to the blue-skinned boy and prostrated himself on the ground at his feet. The boy merely touched Ari's father on his shoulders and urged him to get up.

The fruit offered endless slices, enough to feed every hungry mouth that had gathered around Ari now, enough to fill every outstretched hand that had long forgotten what it felt like to hold a weighty morsel of food, without worrying it would be their last.

In his haste to cut and offer as many slices as fast as he could, Ari nicked his palm. He lifted the fruit, aghast that his blood would mingle with the only food available to the village now. But there was nothing on his palm. Only the blue juice of the fruit had stained his hand. Likely a superficial scrape.

Relieved, he resumed with pride the joyful task of slicing and distributing this strange new fruit, the fruit of life, to all the people in his village. People who had been on the brink of hunger and death, now given a new lease on life.

Ari went to bed a happy child that night. His belly was full. His heart burst with hope and joy.

Jana slept like the little girl that she was, curled up without worrying about crushing their baby brother, Nayo, who fell asleep in his mother's lap.

For the first time in a long time, baby Nayo slept through the night, nourished with milk from his mother's breasts, milk that had gushed forth upon her first bite of the blue fruit.

# CHAPTER 2

# A SLOW METAMORPHOSIS

It wasn't until several days later, long after the blue-skinned mystics had rid the village of drought and famine, that Jana noticed the thin blue band that encircled Ari's neck, reaching like a long necklace all the way down past his chest and just below his navel.

"Look! You're turning blue," she yelled one afternoon as Ari splashed about in the stream with their friends.

Jana had chosen to stay out of the water, claiming she wasn't keen to indulge in child's play. It wasn't the first time she had desisted from joining in their games, but the change in her had been abrupt. Almost overnight. She had been more jovial and friendly during the difficult days of the famine than she was these days, Ari thought. *Leave her be, she's going through one of her moods,* their mother said whenever Ari mentioned to her how aloof Jana had become.

When Jana had opted to sit under the tree instead of jumping into the water with them that afternoon, Ari understood she was in one of her *moods* again, though what that really meant, he still didn't know.

She had brought a book to read but Ari noticed she hadn't turned a single page in the hour he and his friends had spent playing in the water. Instead, she looked at the book, then at the horizon, then back at the book again without really seeing what her eyes perceived. So it came as a surprise to Ari that she was the one to point out the anomaly on his skin.

Ari looked where she was pointing, and sure enough he spotted a thin, blue trail that snaked down his chest, skirted his navel, and climbed back up his chest on the other side. He imagined it forming a loop around the back of his neck. He touched it with his fingers.

"Does it hurt?" Jana asked.

Ari shook his head. He rubbed against his skin, hoping the blue would fade away like cheap ink. It didn't.

The silence at the stream was unsettling. Only a few moments ago, whoops and shouts had filled the air. Now the silent stares of his friends at the blue ribbon that a part of his skin had become was oppressive.

Without warning, Ari scooped a palmful of water and hurled it right at Jana's face. She screamed, then sprang up to drench him, and that broke the hiatus.

The blue mark forgotten momentarily, Ari and Jana and their friends spent the rest of the afternoon splashing about in the stream, which was so full it was impossible to recall the dry trench in the ground it had become before the blue-skinned mystics had come and refilled it with water.

It wasn't until long after the sun had slipped out of sight and the sky had turned so dark it looked like a large, gaping void, one that could suck all the inhabitants of Hanish into its depths were it not for gravity keeping them glued to the land, that Ari slipped out of his home where his mother, father,

Jana, and baby Nayo slept without a care in the world, and made his way by starlight towards the step-well where the blue-skinned mystics had parked their caravans and pitched their tents.

The well was on the outskirts of Hanish, in an area that was once deemed too far away to be exploited to the advantage of the village. Once people had started to die of hunger and thirst, the distance between the village centre and the well had become less daunting.

It hadn't been a real well to begin with. A large, sunken hole in the ground, square-shaped, with steep steps carved into all four sides, the well was thought to be a remnant of an ancient civilization. When it rained, water pooled in its depths. But in between the spells of rain, all the water simply dissipated into the air around them in a matter of days.

Some thought it was a sacred place. An ancient temple of sorts. Some others believed it was haunted. Even water didn't stay there for longer than a few days, they pointed out.

But when all their rivers and streams had run dry, all the villagers had trooped to the ancient well and sought to fill their tiny pans and bowls with its water. When the well dried up, they dug deeper into its depths, but the hard earth had no more water to give them.

That night, the water shimmered and sparkled under the light of a full moon. Ari stood several paces away, hiding behind one of the many strange blue trees that had sprung up all over their village.

The blue-skinned mystics had set up camp on the opposite side of the step-well from where he stood. Their caravans and tents stood in a meticulous line at a distance from the far edge of the well. Little fires flickered in front of the tents and threw dancing shadows into the darkness beyond. What had been a stretch of barren land over the past three years now presented a vast grove, almost a forest, behind the tents.

The mystics sat around their fires in different groups. Mothers with small children gossiped around one of the central fires. Older children, although too young to be awake at this hour of the night, played beside them. A larger group of men and women huddled around the farthest fire. Ari watched as they passed a hookah around. They appeared to be engaged in a lively conversation but from this distance, he couldn't make out what they were saying.

With a deep breath and his heart hammering in his chest, he stepped forward and made his way towards the large group. He had not given any thought to what he would say to the blue-skinned mystics when he saw them. When Jana had noticed how his skin had turned blue, he had only known he couldn't put away a visit to the mystics any longer.

He had noticed the aberration on his skin several days ago although he had pretended otherwise at the stream that morning. In the delight and excitement of play, he had forgotten to keep his tunic on so as to conceal the blue lines that had started to form on his body. He had been so careful all these days, only to slip up that morning.

The first line had appeared on his palm, where he had nicked himself while cutting the first blue fruit borne by the tree that had sprung from the ground, nourished by a drop of his tear.

It hadn't taken long after that for the blueness to turn up on different parts of his body.

On his chest. On his ankles. Under his feet. Never staying in one place for long.

As if a little blue thread were winding its way under his skin, exploring different patches of him to ensconce itself in.

Two days ago, the blue line had wrapped itself around his neck like a noose. He had covered it up by lifting the collar of his tunic and deflecting questions from anyone who questioned him on his choice of a stifling attire on what had turned out to be a rather hot summer day.

This morning was the first time the blue line had grown as long as a necklace. A garland. It was the longest he had ever seen. He didn't know if it meant anything. But now that Jana and the others had begun to notice it, he reckoned it was time to do something about it.

A silence fell upon the group as he approached.

Like a warning.

Ari tried to hold his head high in an attempt to hide his nervousness and uncertainty. But doubt sneaked up his spine. Had he made a mistake coming here?

"Finally!" A voice said. It had come from the group, but Ari could not tell who had spoken.

A figure rose and detached itself from the group and made its way towards him. Only when the person had come within a few feet did Ari recognize the blue-skinned boy who had coaxed a tree to grow the instant he and his tribe had entered the land of Hanish.

Words escaped Ari. The boy was the only blue-skinned mystic he had seen that day. The rest of his tribe had stayed inside their caravans. Ari had not guessed there were children too, so soundless the entourage had been. Even the blue boy who had caught Ari's tear had not spoken a word that day. He had carried out all his magic without a whisper or a sigh.

Ari hadn't seen any of the blue-skinned mystics after that

first day. But he had heard all the rumours about them. How they had filled the village with trees and crops, how they had brought back water to the rivers and the streams. And more importantly, how they had filled the ancient step-well with so much water it would sate the thirst of the people of Hanish for several generations to come.

It was all anybody in the village could talk about. Which is how Ari had known where they had taken up residence.

"We've been waiting for you," the blue-skinned boy said with a smile.

Ari looked up at him. Confused. Yet also curious. Even up close, the boy looked quite like a silhouette. It was the light of the moon that made him glow. Whether that made him look radiant or spooky, Ari couldn't quite make up his mind.

But his voice was gentle. Soft. Almost like Jana's. Which made Ari take an instant liking to him. For he sounded nothing like the older Hanish boys who had gone back to loitering about the village now that their excavation services at the step-well were no longer required.

"You knew I'd come?" Ari's voice sounded like a croak to his own ears.

"It was only a matter of time."

The boy took Ari's hand in his own and led him towards the gathering he had peeled himself away from. In the dancing light cast by the fire they huddled around, their faces were almost purple.

"Welcome, Ari." The man who spoke was bald. Even his scalp was a deep indigo in colour.

Ari approached him and touched his feet in a gesture of respect.

"Stay blessed," the man said, briefly touching the top of Ari's head with his hand. "I take it your skin is turning blue?"

Ari was taken aback. "How did you know?"

"The Great Spirit runs through you," the man said. "It is why a drop of tear from your eyes moved the earth so much she yielded her most precious fruit to you and your kin."

"But that was all *your* magic." Ari looked around for the blue-skinned boy, the one who had drawn the tree out from the soil. The boy stood where Ari had left him. A few paces behind. He smiled.

"Magic does not belong to any one person," the bald man said. "We wield it. We use it. But it belongs to no one. It comes to us of its own volition. The Great Spirit dictates our actions. And it chose to come through you to help the people of your land."

A delightful thrill took root in Ari's belly and rippled outwards, making his heart flutter and his nerves tingle. His memory of the birth of the first life-saving tree that had sprouted in Hanish was incredibly vivid, so deep and lasting an impression the event had left on him. The way a little sprig had uncoiled into a large tree bearing fruits shaped like teardrops. The way Ari had joyfully cut into the everlasting fruit and distributed slices of it to the hungry villagers.

"You have a lot to learn." The bald man's voice nudged Ari out of his thoughts. "There is much you can do for the world, if you choose to, quite like you've done for Hanish."

He beckoned to someone behind Ari. The blue-skinned boy came forth.

"Manaya," the bald man said, "give Ari a glimpse of what he can do."

Manaya bowed to the bald man in affirmation, then took Ari by the hand and led him towards the step-well.

Manaya. Ari sounded the name in his mind, stressing every syllable, and found it to be a source of immense delight. Ma-na-ya.

"What does it mean?" Ari asked.

The boy merely raised an eyebrow.

"Your name. Manaya."

"Nothing that I know of," Manaya replied. "You can call me by any other name, and I'd still be one of the tribe. A wielder of magic. A bearer of healing."

Manaya's answer surprised Ari, who had always taken pride in the fact that his own name was a reference to the lion, the majestic king of the jungle. Not that Ari had ever seen a lion in his entire life. He had only heard tales of the beast whose roar was rumoured to make the forest floor quiver for miles around. For someone like Ari, who detested loud, angry voices, the idea of a single powerful roar to silence anyone who bothered him had always been emancipating.

"My name means lion," Ari said. "I like what it means."

Manaya threw his head back and laughed. Unkindly, it seemed to Ari, who felt affronted. "What's so funny?" he asked.

Manaya put a hand on Ari's shoulder and smiled kindly. "When you find out what you are capable of, you will see you won't need to be a mere lion ever again."

A mere lion? Ari had never heard anyone speak of the king of the jungle in such a frivolous manner.

"Did you know a lion can bite your head off faster than you can say Ari?" He admonished his new friend.

Manaya bit his lower lip to keep from laughing. "That's only if the lion can catch me," he said.

And in an act of demonstration, he collapsed to the ground with a splash.

Ari jumped back, startled.

Manaya's body had transformed into something fluid. Water, perhaps, but Ari couldn't be certain.

Manaya had fallen like a bucketful of water thrown out of an upstairs window. Now, he lay pooled at Ari's feet and flowed towards the edge of the step-well.

"Come. Follow me." It was Manaya's voice alright, soft and kind. But it seemed to come from inside Ari's head.

Manaya, in his new form, slipped over the edge of the well and disappeared into the water.

"Manaya!" Ari shouted frantically. He ran along the side of the well, peering into its depths, looking for his new friend.

The full moon shone brightly on the surface of the water, which was surprisingly calm. There was not even a ripple from which Ari could glean a clue as to Manaya's whereabouts. "Manaya," he shouted again.

"Step into the water," Manaya's voice boomed inside Ari's head once more.

Ari stepped back from the edge of the well. "I can't," he said.

"Why not?"

"I … I don't know how to swim." Surely, it was acceptable that a child who had grown up in a land of famine and drought had not had the opportunity to learn how to swim.

"You don't need to swim," Manaya's voice said again. Gentle. Encouraging. Like a second voice inside Ari's head. A kind one. The voice of the Great Spirit. The one that filled him with love and hope, not with fear and dread.

Ari stepped closer to the edge. He stuck out a foot and dipped his toes in the water. For a brief moment. Quickly, he pulled it back.

The water was cool. Tantalizing. But there was nothing to reveal what lay beneath the surface, what the darkness beneath the reflection of the moon concealed.

"It's just me," the other voice in his head said. "Come."

It seemed a foolhardy thing to do. The stream he bathed in with his friends each morning, ever since the blue-skinned mystics had filled it up with water, was not even knee deep.

But this step-well was a different body of water altogether. So many stories about the well had been told in the village. Sometimes the villagers had revered it as a sacred place. At other times, they had reviled it and deemed it haunted. Inauspicious.

Whatever the grown-ups had had to say about the well, they had delivered those messages like warnings.

*It's a holy place. Stay away.*

*It's an evil place. Stay away.*

The only constant in their messages was that the well was not a place for any sane person, let alone children, to explore.

All that had changed when water had disappeared from their village altogether, when the rainclouds had deemed Hanish unworthy of their offerings, when the snow that melted on the distant mountains did not deign to flow through the village. No place was too sacred or unholy to trespass in their desperate search for water.

Even then, it was only the grown-ups who had been

recruited to dig through the heart of the step-well. Children were still warned away from this place.

It seemed cruel to Ari in that moment that the blue-skinned mystics who had saved the surviving villagers from dying of thirst and hunger had been asked to set up their caravans and pitch their tents here. Right beside the infamous well.

Despite being the saviours of Hanish, the blue-skinned mystics too had to be kept at more than an arm's length. They had to be kept at a sufficient distance. Like a God one worshipped but also feared.

A pang of embarrassment bloomed in Ari's chest and spread throughout his body like wildfire. After all that the blue-skinned mystics had done for Hanish, the villagers had all but treated them like outcasts.

But another thought sneaked into Ari's mind. Were the mystics aware of this? Surely, they were? They were people of magic.

There was the magic he had seen them perform. Like making a land come alive once more.

Which meant they likely also wielded magic that he was not privy to. Could they read thoughts? Intentions? Or manipulate them?

Suddenly, coming here to meet them all by himself didn't seem like a great idea anymore. No one at home knew where he was. If baby Nayo woke up their mother or father in the middle of the night, surely they would notice he was missing. And that would throw them into panic, he was certain.

"I have to go," he called out to Manaya, looking in the general direction of the water.

Manaya did not reply, neither out loud nor in his mind.

Ari wasn't sure if Manaya had heard him, but it didn't matter anymore. All he wanted was to go back home to his mother and father, to Jana, and to baby Nayo.

He turned on his heel but before he could take a step away from the water, a dark silhouette rushed at him, bursting forth from the paler darkness of the night.

Two hands planted themselves on his chest and pushed him back.

The last thing Ari noticed before the step-well swallowed him up was the way the head of the figure curved, like the underside of a pot.

Whoever had pushed him was bald.

# CHAPTER 3

# SHADES OF BLUE

Blue was the colour of the sky. Whether at midnight or in the afternoon. Unless grey clouds dragged a veil over it, an occurrence that had been so rare in Hanish for several years that the villagers had held little hope for it to happen.

Blue was the colour of the mysterious people who had come to save the land of Hanish from eternal ruin. Theirs was the kind of blue that was neither pale nor dark, but a bright, saturated shade. Sapphire, one of the older folks in the village had said, but Ari had never seen a sapphire stone. But seeing how the mystics' skin appeared full of life, he thought that such a stone would look very pretty indeed.

Blue was said to be the colour of the eyes of the people who lived in the far north, in a land that was so cold and dark it leached all colour out of people's skin. It was said that all the light of the sky had settled into the irises of their eyes, which were a piercing blue, so they could see clearly even if the sun made no appearance for days on end.

Blue was the colour baby Nayo had once turned at his

edges by the time Ari could return from the neighbouring village with a pitcher full of water. His fingertips. His toes. The tip of his nose. Everything had turned blue. As if all the life in him was ebbing, receding to his edges, and waiting for the slightest chance to slip out and away from him.

Blue was the colour of the water in this step-well the only time Ari had caught a glimpse of it in daylight, having lost his way one afternoon.

He had been only five years old at the time. It was the summer before the drought had set in. Mother had sent him to deliver a bundle of bread and cooked vegetables, tied in a square piece of cloth only slightly bigger than her palm, to father who was at work in the fields on the outskirts of the village.

Ari hadn't lost his way but had somehow wandered towards the step-well that all the grown-ups talked about as if it had once been among their favourite haunts but forbade children from ever going near it. He couldn't explain what had drawn him towards it.

He hadn't even known the way, but something, something like the whisper of the wind or the call of a bird or the sound of the earth sighing, had drawn him westwards, and he hadn't even known where it was leading him until he stepped beyond a thicket of oaks and the step-well appeared in front of him like a sheet of blue sky spread out on the ground.

It was evening by the time Ari's hungry and irate father and half the village found him sitting by the side of the step-well, staring into its depths. Mesmerized. Hypnotized.

Ari had no recollection of this incident at all even though Jana had reminded him often enough how Mother had sat by the stove, wringing her hands and burning the food she was meant to be cooking, until Jana realized she too would go hungry that evening if she didn't intervene.

Blue was the colour of the teardrop fruit that now bloomed all over Hanish. Its skin was a deep, dark blue, and so was its pulpy interior flesh.

Blue was the colour the line on Ari's palm had begun to turn a few days after he had accidentally nicked it while cutting the first teardrop fruit. The juice of the fruit had stained his palm blue for a few days, the way mulberries painted his fingertips purplish when he plucked them. The blue stains hadn't concerned him, not even when most of them disappeared and only the gash where he had nicked himself had turned a purplish blue. He had inspected his bruises and picked at scabs often enough to discern the strange colours wounds first turned into before the skin healed.

Blue was the colour of Manaya, a kind being Ari had taken a liking to since they first met, with the entire village watching with great anticipation the kind of magic the blue-skinned mystics were rumoured to be capable of.

Blue was the colour of the bald man, the leader of the tribe, whom Ari had met only a little while ago, who had enthralled Ari with his soft voice but loud words, words that had filled Ari's head with the notion that he was someone special because the Great Spirit coursed through him, even though Ari hadn't quite grasped its implication, what it meant to be a wielder of magic.

Blue was the colour of the same bald man who had deemed Ari special only to push him into the step-well, a site revered and reviled in equal measures by the villagers of

Hanish, a large, terraced pond of water that was now devouring Ari for he was surely drowning.

Blue, Ari imagined, for he had squeezed his eyes shut, unwilling to watch himself die, was the colour of his last breath that was being forced out of his mouth now in a flurry of bubbles, big and small, as water seeped into his lungs and rendered further breath impossible.

CHAPTER 4

# A LESSON IN CONTRASTS

Ari couldn't see himself when he came to. He opened his eyes, or at least that was what he thought he had done, for he could now *see* around him. Water jiggled all around, tossing him about like a feather adrift on a light breeze.

The bottom of the well was surprisingly clear. Ari had never given much thought to what lay at the bottom of the well, but he hadn't expected it to be empty and devoid of underwater creatures. Weren't there supposed to be fish? And algae?

Storytellers in the village often talked of strange creatures, not necessarily monsters, that were rumoured to lurk at the bottom of the step-well.

But there was nothing here. Even the bottom was a flat, undisturbed patch of muddy ground that didn't seem to register his presence, for nothing except the water stirred as he moved closer to the bottom and drew back.

He wanted to stick out a toe and press the earth to feel how firm or loose it was. Only, when he attempted to, he discovered he no longer had toes. Or feet. Or legs, for that matter.

He looked down, in a manner of speaking, for how could you look up or down if you were somehow missing a head in the first place?

Ari didn't know it yet, the fact of his missing head, but what he saw was that he no longer had a body. No limbs. No hands to grasp something with. No feet to take him here or there.

He attempted to raise a hand to feel his face but there were no hands to obey his commands. No hands to feel whether the rest of his body still existed in its corporeal form or not. Not even the blue-tinted one.

Surely, he was still in possession of his eyes? He could *see* all the water around him, even if he could not see his own body, although the sensations of wriggling his fingers and toes were as real as the water that flowed all around him.

He must have died, Ari was certain now. He was now that spirit that must have abandoned his body.

He looked around, wondering if he'd spot his own corpse. Would his father come to look for him? Would he think to search in the depths of this well?

Ari moved with surprising and graceful ease. To say that he moved was, perhaps, quite misleading. Movement implied an action with limbs. A flailing of arms. A thrashing of legs. A forceful pushing against the water to make it move, creating a passageway for him to traverse.

But he was certain he was disembodied. He had become something else. What it was, he couldn't say.

But whatever he now was, was not encased in a human body, his eight-year-old body with blue lines threading through brown skin. An interlacing of sky and earth. Of water and soil. Of the elements that nourished and sustained life.

"At last," the voice in his head piped up again. Manaya's voice. Emerging from somewhere deep inside Ari. As if it were his own voice, calling out to him like a friend would.

"Where are you? What has happened to me?" Ari was surprised he could speak aloud but the words were out of his mouthless mouth before he could pause to consider what else he could possibly do in this incorporeal form.

He spun around, in so far as his gaze travelled from left to right in a full circle and came back to rest on the same spot as far as he could tell, for everything around him looked identical here. Underwater. A series of steps leading up, up, and up as far as he could see.

Something rippled in the water around him. An invisible fish darting out of sight. The space just beyond the corner of his eye bending, shimmering, altering somehow. Becoming more fluid. Less substantial. More ethereal.

He turned to look at it only to find whatever had been there, shining, twinkling, had moved too, just out of reach. Like something always meant to be on the fringes.

"This is who we are," Manaya's voice said. "Nothing. And everything. Both at once."

Manaya's words confused Ari, who wanted nothing more than to see his friend, see himself, peer into a mirror and find out what had happened to him.

"That makes no sense," Ari said.

"It is not meant to," Manaya chuckled. "This is what the Great Spirit is. A flow of energy. Infinite. Indiscriminating. Flowing everywhere it can. It just is."

"The Great Spirit," Ari said slowly, as it occurred to him, "the Great Spirit that you speak of, it is life, isn't it?"

"Life, yet so much more. It is the very fabric of the cosmos, the thread that weaves through every living being, the unseen force that governs the birth of the new and the death of the old, for what lives must eventually die, make way for other forms of life to manifest and flourish."

"Surely then it flows through everyone, through every living being?"

"You would think so," Manaya said. "It is most vibrant in nature. The Great Spirit throbs in the heart of every non-human being. In humans, it has become sullied. Tainted by abuse. Humankind's desire to control their lives and this world has disconnected them from the very essence their lives are made of."

"How come I still have it then?"

"Children are different." Manaya's voice held a very distinct smile. "Not yet trained in the grown-up ways of the world."

Ari thought about this for a few moments. A bubble of pride swelled up inside him, but only for a moment. "Why not Jana then? Why not Nayo?"

"You have many questions," Manaya said.

"Is that wrong?"

"Why would that be wrong?"

"I don't know." Ari phantom-shrugged. "My father or mother don't always like me asking so many questions. Whenever I ask them anything, they tell me to go play with my friends."

Manaya laughed. "They must have either been preoccupied with something or didn't know the answers themselves."

Ari considered this for a few moments. "But grown-ups always have all the answers, don't they?"

"Our tribe has travelled all over the world," Manaya said. "Human beings everywhere are identical in this aspect. There is only one truth. It is that the Great Spirit is unfathomable. When we try to analyze and describe it, define it using shapes and forms and colours and sounds, we can explain only a part of it. But never all of it. But wherever we go, we've seen that grown-ups can't bear not knowing."

"Not knowing what?"

"The future. The past. The world around them. Other people. The nature of time and space. The nature of animals and people. They want to arm themselves with knowledge, as if that alone would ward off calamity or death, but the Great Spirit is beyond intellectual comprehension. So no, grown-ups do not always have all the answers even if they wish they did."

Manaya's words unsettled Ari. Wasn't it always his father or mother who had the solution to every problem they faced? Weren't the older boys who got up to no good wiser than he was in the ways of the world? If growing up didn't get you all the answers, what good was it anyway?

"And your people have all the answers?" Ari asked.

Manaya chuckled. "Of course not! They don't wish to either. They have long stopped asking any questions about the Great Spirit and life and the world and its mysteries. When you stop asking the questions, the answers reveal themselves, but by then you don't need them anyway."

Ari was confused. Manaya had begun to sound like Ari's father did. Esoteric. Resorting to wordplay. Especially when he didn't want to supply a direct answer to Ari's question. Or when he didn't know the answer, Ari thought alongside.

"You didn't answer one of my questions," Ari said.

"Which one?"

"Why did your leader say that the Great Spirit flows through me? Why not through Jana? Or Nayo?"

"Nayo is an infant. His bodily needs must be addressed first before he can help wield magic."

"And Jana?"

Manaya did not respond for a few moments. In the stillness of the water around them, Ari couldn't be certain if Manaya was still with him or not. He asked again, "What about Jana?"

"Jana too has worldly desires and needs to be fulfilled," Manaya replied.

"What does that mean?"

"Come with me."

"Come where?"

There was no response. It appeared as if Manaya had already left for wherever he was headed.

"And how? How do I move?"

Manaya did not reply but something like a wave pushed Ari gently from the top. He found himself drifting through the well, heading downwards, all the way to the muddy bottom, and just as he expected to slam into it, he went right through it.

Through the soil he trickled and crept, like a drop of water, flowing this way and that, strangely not absorbed by anything he touched or that touched him.

It was like swimming, but nothing like what Ari had imagined swimming would be. It was more like flowing. A crawling, perhaps. Ari felt himself tremble a little bit, but without a body to pull, he couldn't really be creeping and crawling, could he?

On and on he went, not of his own volition for he knew not where he was to go, but something in him knew what he didn't and directed him there.

Under the ground. Through the soil. Past worms and underground creatures. Past the thick roots of the blue-fruit trees that the mystics had called forth from the earth so that the people of Hanish would never run out of food to eat.

Above, the soft footsteps of foxes hunting for prey. The hoot of an owl in the distance. Another, right above him, calling back in response. Faraway stars humming as they twinkled, their light from years ago slicing through space and time to reach the earth.

"Stop!" Manaya's voice was unexpectedly close. Ari jumped, as best as he could in this formless form, feeling the same jolt of fear he had experienced when Jana had pointed to the garland of blue skin on his body only that afternoon.

He was still underground. Rich, fragrant earth pressed on him from all sides, but he didn't find it suffocating or limiting in any way. Why would he, given how easily he could move through it, as if earth was air?

"Let's go up," Manaya said.

Ari thought of moving up, and the very consideration propelled him up out of the soil and into the root of a tree. And now he was the force of life that passed from the earth to the tree, up its roots, up its trunk.

And now that he was above the ground, the darkness around him was less dense, less absolute somehow, made pale by the light of the moon and yesterday's stars. The sweet, decadent scent of the earth was also less obvious here, diluted by the fresh, crisp air of the cool night.

And now he was the force of life thrumming through the branch of the tree, a teardrop tree—what else could it have been, there were so many of them in Hanish now—and now he was one of its leaves, a flat, broad, heart-shaped leaf whose tip curled into a small tendril.

He hung at the edge of the tendril. He *was* the edge of the tendril.

And from here, when he stopped marvelling at the way with which he had become the tip of a leaf of one of the many strange, magic-filled, life-saving trees in the village of Hanish, and turned his attention outwards, he heard noises.

Muffled. Indistinct, at first. Not the soft tread of animals on a nocturnal forage. Not the rustling of creatures hiding or stalking in the bushes.

But something like a soft, rhythmic sweep. Something brushing against a bed of leaves.

Ari looked around but the night gave nothing away.

Mixed into those sounds were voices. Breathy, raspy voices. Definitely human. Not uttering any distinct words. But moans and throaty growls. Soft and hushed at first, but slowly growing louder despite themselves.

And there, in the one place he had not peered at, right underneath him, lay the sources of the unfamiliar sounds.

A tangle of limbs. A thick mop of black curls, tumbling over another face concealed beneath. A long, lean body, wrapped around another beneath. Clothes scattered around them, discarded like props not required for this scene.

The two of them, rocking in unison, back and forth, back and forth, their breaths and moans gathering speed and tempo, like that part of a musical score that requires deft fingers to fly over strings and keys faster than light, until they no longer can.

A shudder. The air around him trembled. The leaf he was on, the leaf he was part of, shivered.

A muffled groan. A suppressed wail. Bounced off the tree trunks and echoed faintly all around them.

The dance stopped. The music faded. Time ceased to exist.

After what felt like eternity, a cloud dragged itself away from the moon. And the body on top peeled itself away to reveal who lay beneath.

A pair of eyes looked up at Ari. Wide with shock and wonder. Glinting like silver jewels in the moonlight.

A pair of eyes more familiar to him than his own. For he had looked into them more often than he had ever looked into his own in the mirror.

Even though whoever saw the two of them together never failed to remark how they had identical eyes, their mother's eyes, almond-shaped, brown as the earth after the first rainfall.

For those were Jana's eyes.

CHAPTER 5

# INNOCENCE LOST

Ari pulled himself away from the tendril edge of the leaf, scurried through the branch and the tree trunk, down to its root and slipped into the earth, then darted back the way he had come, not pausing for even an instant as he flowed through the soil, until he burst out of the floor of the step-well and swam up and up, then pulled himself out and collapsed beside the edge of the water.

For a long time he lay there, gasping on the ground, his breath coming out in sharp, rapid bursts, hollow and insubstantial. Not enough to fill his lungs.

But the exertion of it tired him and he involuntarily curled himself into a foetal position, folding his legs to his chest and wrapping his arms around his knees, as if tucking himself into an eggshell, keeping his eyes squeezed shut, so he would see nothing of the world outside and nothing from the world outside would lay its eyes on him.

It took him a while to realize that his hands were dry, and when he curled into himself, he felt warm and safe.

With a jolt, he came out of his cocoon and stood up. He

found that he could stand up now, for he was back in his body.

His hands and legs had come back. He lifted his hands—were they blue or brown, he couldn't tell in the light of the night with the moon momentarily obscured by wayward clouds—and put them to his face. He could feel his skin. He could feel the tears that had made his eyes and cheeks damp.

He looked around, as if seeking a witness, someone who could validate his return to an existence in this physical form.

The place was deserted. All the members of the tribe of blue-skinned beings had retreated into their tents and caravans. The campfires had died out. Not even a wisp of smoke remained.

A splash in the water beside him. He jumped back. Something crawled out of the water and crept on to the land. And then it bulged and swelled, then rose, like a wilting stem dragging itself up and willing itself to stand upright once more so that the flower it carried on its tip could unfurl. Manaya.

Ari ran up to Manaya bearing the burden of countless questions.

"What is happening?" Ari asked, while at the same time Manaya said, "Don't worry. We weren't seen."

It took Ari a moment to understand what Manaya was referring to. The memory of Jana looking up at him, eyes wide with wonder and astonishment, as if she couldn't quite believe what had transpired, rushed back into his mind.

Manaya led Ari by the arm to the nearest tree. The two boys sat beside each other and looked out at the water and the night beyond, each lost in his own thoughts but assured of each other's presence.

"What Jana saw," Manaya finally began, "was the tree and

its leaves and its fruits in the light of the moon and the stars, nothing more. When we take the form of the Great Spirit, which is formless, nothing but life itself, we become invisible to most human beings. Especially those who are immersed in this physical world they live in."

Ari let Manaya's words sink in. He had already understood this to some extent, he realized now, that when he had become everything and nothing at once, he had become nothing especially discernible to the world around him too.

That wasn't why he had scampered back. He hadn't been afraid that Jana may have spotted him.

It was the look on her face that had frightened him. The explosion of emotions. Pain and pleasure. Surprise, yet contentment. An expansion, and also a release. How could such stark opposites coexist?

"And what was it that I saw?" Ari whispered. His eyes were fixed on the horizon but all he could see was the sheen of sweat on Jana's face glistening in the moonlight.

He had sometimes seen the same look on the faces of other girls, older girls, who let those boys, those almost-men, kiss them on their lips and on other parts of their body. Ari had never understood what it meant, and it had never once occurred to him that he might one day see the same expression on his sister's face.

"What you saw is how life is made," Manaya spoke, slower and softer than usual, which irked Ari, who wanted to know everything immediately. He didn't want Manaya of all people to tread carefully, resort to wordplay, or do anything that was an attempt at blurring the truth.

"What you saw is how people make love," Manaya continued. "It is what animals do too. A union of two bodies, of the Great Spirit that flows in those two bodies. And when the time is right, a whole new life comes into being."

"A baby, you mean?"

"Yes, this is how babies are made."

"But why does Jana need to make babies now?" Ari cried out. "We already have baby Nayo at home, and even though your people have made sure Hanish will never run out of food, there are enough mouths to feed in our family."

"Not all acts of love-making bring forth a baby," Manaya explained. "Often, people make love simply to express their love for one other."

Ari was still confused. If it took an act of making love to bring a baby into this world, did his mother and father too engage in such a deed? Is that how baby Nayo was born? And Jana? And he too? Was he also a consequence of lovemaking, a child who was infused with the Great Spirit that once flowed in his parents?

"What are you thinking?" Manaya asked.

Ari shook his head. "I don't know." And that was the truth. He didn't know. Confusion and concern grappled for space within his being. Was making love a good thing? Or bad? He didn't know where to slot this newfound knowledge, whether to place it in the category of right and moral deeds or in the category of wrong and immoral. "I don't know," he muttered again.

"It is the way of nature," Manaya said, as if reading his thoughts. "There is nothing good or bad, right or wrong about it. It just is. And it can be a beautiful thing, you know?"

Ari turned sharply to look at Manaya. "Then why do it all hush-hush? In hiding? In places where others wouldn't see?"

"Because the only way you can find your own self is when you're not being watched," Manaya said.

Ari jumped up. "You know what? You're beginning to sound just like my father. With all these cryptic lines that could mean any damn thing you want them to mean. Anything and nothing at all. Just like you and the rest of your tribe. Like that bald leader of yours who pushed me into the water, knowing I would drown."

Ari paused here, searching for a flicker of surprise on Manaya's face. But there was nothing.

"You knew?" Ari gasped. "You knew! You knew he'd do such a thing. And you didn't warn me!"

Ari spun on his heels and ran away. Away from Manaya. Away from the step-well. Away from the tribe of blue-skinned mystics. And back towards the heart of Hanish, towards home, towards his mother and father and baby Nayo and Jana. His breath caught in his throat at the thought of Jana.

The night was at its darkest when Ari slipped into his hut noiselessly. His father's snores could be heard several feet outside the hut. His mother was fast asleep. Hers was the sleep of the exhausted. But not restful, for it left much to desire.

Baby Nayo had begun to stir, which meant Mother would be up soon. Ari slipped under his sheets just as baby Nayo started to wail and Mother jumped up and put her infant to her breast even before she could rub her eyes open, then sank back against the wall, as if hoping to sleep some more. Father turned around and away from his wife and infant son, then resettled himself into a more comfortable position and resumed snoring.

Jana was not in her cot, Ari knew, but there was a lump

under her blanket. Ari stuck out a hand and reached under the blanket. No legs. Only a tufty mass of pillows and sheets.

He stayed awake until Jana slipped into the hut.

Luckily for her, their mother and baby Nayo had both fallen asleep by then, mother still sitting up against the wall, her head lolling forward in sleep, and Nayo asleep in her lap. Their father still snored loudly enough to wake up the sun.

Jana crept in like a shadow. Quiet. Unobserved. She went straight to her cot and disappeared under the blanket.

Only Ari could smell the fragrance of the teardrop tree on her.

# CHAPTER 6

# QUESTIONS AND ACCUSATIONS

It was a yell that roused Ari the next morning.

At first, he thought he was the one yelling, for he was still caught in the throes of a nightmare in which he was drowning, had already sunk deep into the step-well, but was somehow able to shout out loud and call for help.

But the voice he heard now was not his — it came from somewhere outside of him — although the yelling remained loud and distinct. Too close for comfort. He jumped out of bed to find his parents looking at him as if he were dead.

"What have you done?" his father said at the same time that mother demanded to know, "Who did this to you?"

The realization that one question was an accusation while the other was an assumption of his innocence made him laugh. He threw his head back and laughed even before he could consider how inappropriate that could be.

A stinging slap landed across his cheek, and he fell back on his cot. Stunned. His ears were ringing.

He brought one hand up to his cheek, and that's when he

saw how blue his hand had become. His entire hand. No, his entire arm.

He looked at his other hand. Blue.

He shook himself free from the sheets that were tangled around his legs. Limbs, long and blue. The colour of a peacock's feathers.

There was once a God who wore a peacock feather in his crown and who was blue and who was so charming the entire village fell in love with him, Ari recalled a story his mother used to tell him and Jana often when they were younger.

Ari jumped out of the cot, stood up, lifted up his shirt to check. Blue.

No longer a single thread or band of blue snaking across his body. But an explosion of blue. An immersion into the colour of twilight and the colour of dawn. As if he had fallen into a tub of midnight blue and had emerged, dyed in that colour. The colour of the teardrop fruit.

Beyond the sound of his ears ringing, he heard his father yell repeatedly, "What have you done?", and he heard his mother yell at her husband, "How dare you hit my boy!"

Baby Nayo wailed, distressed by the commotion in the hut. Jana was the only one staring at him in silence, although her expression spoke louder than words ever could. It was a look of utter terror. She was petrified for him.

It was Jana's look of fear that unravelled Ari, and he started to cry. Through his tears he saw his father approach him with his arm raised, ready to strike his son once more.

Ari crossed his arms in front of his face in defence.

"Manaya," he wailed. "Manaya did this to me."

# CHAPTER 7

# HALF-TRUTHS FOR ANSWERS

The village chief of Hanish looked at Ari for a long time. Unlike the stories people told of him, Ari found that the old man looked very kind. And very sad.

He reminded Ari of his own grandmother who had given up the ghost in this very hut, on the very cot the village chief now sat upon, although Ari remembered little of her passing away. All his memories of her were of the times she slipped sweetmeats into his little hands when his mother or father were not looking.

The village chief was dressed in rich robes. A bejewelled turban sat on his head. Long wispy locks of silvery grey hair flowed from under his turban and curled around his neck. He sported a thick moustache and a beard, both the colour of his hair.

His eyes were a liquid green, paler than Ari remembered them to be, which made Ari wonder when he had last seen the village chief. At his granddaughter's funeral, Ari realized with a gasp.

The village chief moved his head sharply to meet Ari's eyes. Ari didn't look away. "I am sorry about Sheila," he said.

Words that he had been taught to say at Sheila's cremation. Words he had not been able to coax out of his mouth when he had tagged along with his father, mother, Jana and baby Nayo to pay their condolences to the chief after the rituals had concluded.

Every living person in the village, weak or new-born, ailing or disabled, had attended the cremation. Everybody had walked along with Sheila's father, the son of the village chief, all the way from his home, a large assortment of huts over-looking a yard in the centre, where the chief met with his people when the weather was in their favour, to the cremation grounds on the other side of the village, quite close to the step-well.

Ari and Jana had both been exhausted by the time they reached the grounds. On the one occasion he chose to whine to his mother, she had shushed him and hissed in his ear that he ought to be grateful that *he* was at least alive.

Even so, when Ari saw Sheila's father lay her shrouded corpse on the pyre and light it with a burning torch, when he heard the whoosh of the flames as the fire tore into his dead friend's body, he wished he had been the one to die.

When they had stepped up to the mourning parents to pay their condolences, he had stayed mum because he was not sorry that Sheila had died. He had been happy for her, happy that she wouldn't have to bear another moment of being admonished by the grown-ups for the way she sat or talked or ate or complained or frowned.

And now, standing in front of the village chief, Ari

couldn't help but feel sorry for the old man, sorry for Sheila at last, for it was true that she was taken away too soon.

"Tell me about Manaya," the village chief said.

Ari spoke to him about how he had accidentally cut his palm while distributing the first teardrop fruit to the villagers, how he had noticed the first thread of blue weave its way in and out of his skin, appearing on his hand one day, only to disappear and surface on his chest the next morning.

He spoke about how he had tried to keep the recurring blueness hidden under his garments but had inadvertently given himself away yesterday afternoon while playing in the stream with Jana and his friends.

Yesterday afternoon? Here he paused, wondering if it had been only yesterday when Jana had noticed the blue band on his skin.

So much had happened since.

Ari remembered the faraway look in Jana's eyes, that look of distraction, of being there beside the stream yet somewhere else at the same time. It occurred to him her head must have been filled with thoughts of that older boy she had met with last night.

How long had she been carrying on with him? Did their mother and father know? Of course not! If they got wind of it, Jana would be locked up in the hut or married off to the first man willing to make her his bride.

Ari shuddered at the thought. The village chief cleared his throat, which dragged Ari back to reality.

He spoke with renewed vigour about how he thought that the blue-skinned mystics would be the ones to help him get rid of the blue marks on his skin. Surely, they'd know something about these things.

He talked about making his way to the step-well where they had put up, about meeting the boy who had used Ari's tears to bring the first teardrop tree out of an infertile earth.

Here Ari felt a stab of guilt, because, after all, these people had helped his village, had saved his family and the rest of the village from becoming extinct by starvation.

But he had begun this story, he had blamed Manaya for what had happened, and now Ari had no choice but to continue with this narrative.

Ari then spoke about meeting Manaya and some of the members of the tribe, about how their bald leader had talked to him of the Great Spirit that throbbed in Ari's veins, how Manaya had led him to the step-well and slinked into it, how Ari too had stepped into the water—

"What were you thinking? You could have drowned!" This was his father, who was no doubt burning with shame at all that his son had been up to behind his back and at the fact that he was learning of his son's doings only now, in the presence of the village chief, for goodness' sake. It must have taken him great restraint to keep from thrashing his son.

Ari flinched, expecting a blow, feeling a blow that was not delivered physically in that moment but which brought to memory how his father had struck him that morning. He recalled all the beatings his father had given him for as long as he could remember.

"Does your father beat you?" the village chief asked, and Ari was so shocked at the brazenness of this question that he burst into tears.

Beside him, his father fell to his knees and folded his hands and begged, "Forgive me, Sir, but the boy seems to get more and more impudent by the day."

The village chief narrowed his eyes at Ari's father and said in a voice that was cold and menacing. "Chandra, I will not tolerate violence anywhere in my village. Even within the four walls of your hut. You will do well to remember this for life."

Ari's father prostrated himself and touched the village chief's feet. "Forgive me, Sir, it will never happen again."

"It is not my forgiveness you need," the village chief said, pulling back his feet. He gestured towards Ari.

Ari's father looked up at the village chief with great incredulity. He looked at his son, and Ari saw in his father's eyes a mixture of fear and hatred and disbelief. For who had ever heard of a father falling at his son's feet and begging for mercy?

And what punishment would be meted out to Ari, for surely his father would blame him for the embarrassment he had suffered in the presence of the village chief?

Ari began to tremble. The village chief said, "Fear not, my child. No harm will come to you, I promise you this."

And he turned to look at Ari's father, who looked like he wanted to spew a thousand angry words, shatter a thousand worlds into pieces, but knew better than to attempt such an act of insolence in the presence of the man who could banish him and his family from the only home they had ever known in all their lives.

And so, Ari's father bit his tongue and crawled towards him, touched his son's feet briefly, as fleetingly as he could, with only his fingertips, and mumbled an apology that Ari could neither hear nor comprehend.

But it didn't matter. Ari wanted to get away from his father, he wanted his father to get away from him, and he wanted the village chief to stay in this hut forever and not leave him with his father ever again.

Ari watched as his father peeled himself away and went to stand against the wall at the back of the hut, a very different man, a defeated man now, who wore the same look on his face that Ari had seen on Jana's yesterday afternoon at the stream. As if something had been taken away from him forever, and he would spend the rest of his life looking for it on the horizon.

The village chief turned towards Ari. "What happened when you stepped into the water? Were you not afraid?"

An image of a shadowy figure, a silhouette in the darkness, rose in Ari's mind. The image of a bald, blue-skinned person thrusting Ari back into the water with his hands, refusing to let the young lad do what any sensible eight-year-old would have done, walk away from the well, especially if he didn't know how to swim.

Ari gulped, and the words that came out of his mouth were strangled by their own half-true nature. "I began to turn away from the step-well, but then I slipped and fell into the water."

The village chief narrowed his eyes at Ari, who was certain that the wise, old man could read his thoughts. The boy ploughed on. "But I did not drown. I became ..." And here he had to pause again, for what was it he had become? Nothing? And how could he explain something that was nothing in the first place?

"What did you become, child?" the village chief coaxed him once more.

"I don't know." Ari shrugged. "Manaya said I was nothing and everything at the same time."

The village chief nodded as if in comprehension, and that

encouraged Ari to continue, whether or not the words he used felt adequate enough to describe his adventure.

Yes! That is what it had been. An adventure. Like the ones children in books have. Dangerous, risky adventures they come out of using their wit. Oh, the pride that swelled in Ari's chest at this shift in perspective!

"It was actually very exciting," he said. "I could swim, even though I couldn't see my own limbs anymore. I could seep through the earth, and I rose through the root of a teardrop tree and climbed all the way through its trunk to its branches and fruits and leaves. It was as if I was that root. That branch. That fruit. That leaf. The very tip of that leaf."

"Which tree was this?"

"The largest one among that cluster in the thick of the jungle where—"

Jana stiffened beside him perceptibly. What had Ari been about to say? That cluster of trees where the older boys of the village gathered to get up to no good?

He and Jana had spied on them, the older kids, almost grown-up men in some ways, watched them blow rings of smoke out of their still-pink lips.

Often, he had gone alone to watch them, especially when one of them brought a girlfriend along and they did unspeakable things, things for which Ari had not had words to describe until now — lovemaking, that's what Manaya had said, life-making — never once imagining that it would be Jana one day he'd find in the arms of one of those bad, almost-men boys.

"Which cluster of trees?" the village chief asked. Clearly, he had begun to figure out when Ari tended to stall and needed some goading to continue.

"The cluster just out of sight of the step-well," Ari said, referring to a location that was nowhere near where he had seen Jana or anyone else.

Jana exhaled softly. The village chief cast a quick glance at her, and Ari worried he'd prod her next.

"There was no one there," Ari said hastily. "It was the dead of the night, and … and … I am sorry I know I shouldn't have been out there too, it's just … it's just that I followed Manaya and I didn't know what was happening."

Yet another half-truth. Ari had simply gone along with Manaya in the beginning. But hadn't there been a moment, several moments in fact, when he had been more intentional about where he wanted to go, what he wanted to explore in his new form of nothingness?

The village chief nodded, and Ari continued, "I could see the night, the moon and the stars, all the trees around us. Then we came back the same way. When we got out of the step-well, I was back in this form. Except, I didn't know my skin had turned all blue. Until this morning when—"

He turned to look behind his shoulder but stopped, not wanting to draw more attention to the fact that his father had struck him not very long ago.

Instead, Ari looked down at his feet, a resplendent blue against the dark, muddy brown of the floor of the hut.

It was a familiar sight, he remembered now.

# CHAPTER 8

# WHAT DOES YOUR GODDESS LOOK LIKE?

Ari was four years old. It was the first full moon of the year. The village of Hanish had come alive to celebrate the birth of the village deity, Hanadevi, after whom the village was named.

A temple dedicated to Hanadevi stood at the entrance to the village. It sheltered a large idol of the Goddess, who stood tall, taller than any human being had ever dared to be in Hanish. A simple crown adorned her head, and her long hair flowed down to her waist.

The Goddess had appeared overnight.

For as long as anyone could remember, the patch of land by the village border had long remained empty and unused.

And then one day the idol had simply appeared. Firmly installed upon an altar that had risen from the earth in the dead of the night.

In less than a week, the villagers had erected a large temple of stone around the miracle that had manifested and blessed their land.

Made of indigo blue stone, Hanadevi had four arms. In

one hand, she held a spear. In another, a white lotus. The priests never replaced the flower. Every time one wilted, a new bloom appeared in its place of its own accord.

In a third hand, she held a conch. It was rumoured that if you could get close enough to the Goddess and whispered your heart's true desires into the conch, the deity would make your wishes come true.

But of course, the self-appointed priests of the village ensured that nobody but themselves was permitted into the inner sanctum. They alone bore the responsibility of bathing the idol in milk every morning and dressing her up in new garments, before throwing open the doors of the temple for the villagers to visit and pray.

All that had ceased when the drought stole the last of their food and water.

The priests convinced themselves and everyone else that Hanadevi would want the villagers to use their last morsel of food and their last drop of milk to feed their children and not offer them to a stone sculpture who, if they really paused to think about it, had little need for human food to survive.

In the fourth hand of the deity was an object no one could ever describe. It was ensconced in her palm, her fingers curved in a half-fist. Some guessed it to be a marble, for it occasionally shone blue and green when sunlight bounced off it.

It took a few days after the Goddess first appeared for the priests to notice the inky patch that bloomed on the floor right under her fourth hand. It took a few more days of observation and inspection to find out that the object in the hand of the Goddess steadily and unobtrusively dripped a blue liquid to the floor.

No one knew what it was. It was more viscous than ink, almost as thick as blood.

One of the more scholarly priests, who prided on his education and travels across the world, shared his knowledge of the term *'blue blood'* used to refer to a higher social class in some cultures. The others promptly decided that the Goddess had blue blood running through her stone veins, which made the land and the people of Hanish even more blessed than they had believed themselves to be.

The priests placed a copper pot under the Goddess's hand. Not another drop of her precious blood was to be squandered.

It took several days for the pot to be filled to its brim. But it didn't overflow. Blue drops continued to drip into the pot with regularity, but not one spilled over. It was as if the pot had infinite capacity.

After the initial astonishment, the pot was left untouched for a while. Like a miracle best not meddled with.

Until a new year was born and brought with it the first full moon and festivities to worship and celebrate the Goddess of Hanish.

Ari was four years old that year. Along with the other young children of the village, he was taken to the temple to be dressed up like the Goddess.

At the break of dawn, after feeding those hungry little mouths, all the mothers and fathers of the four-year-olds in the village had gathered outside the temple and stripped their little ones to their undergarments.

The sun shone warm and generously over them. The children were only too happy to not be burdened with too many clothes. The people of Hanish took the favourable weather as a good omen, a sign that Hanadevi was pleased with their undertaking.

They painted their children blue. The priests had poured the blue liquid from the copper pot into a large vat (yet the copper pot could not be emptied), so generous had the deity been in gifting her blue blood to them.

The mothers and fathers of the chosen children — chosen because one of the priests had claimed that the deity had appeared in his dreams and had promised to come and bless the village with her presence in the form of a four-year-old — dipped pieces of cloth in the vat and smeared the blue liquid over their little ones' bodies.

Every exposed patch of skin was painted blue. Every parent wanted their child to be the instrument chosen by the deity to appear in Hanish in mortal form, even though no one really knew what consequences that would entail. No price was too small to pay to be touched by God.

The children were delighted. For once, they were permitted to splash about in a blue bath, roll about in blue mud, with no one to reprimand them or drag them to the stream for a cleansing bath.

And when the paint had dried, the children were dressed in robes that sparkled and shone in the brightest of colours. Sizzling reds. Pinks that exploded. Greens that were richer than baby leaves in springtime. Yellows that outshone the sun. Blues that looked like they had been stolen from the skies.

Ari couldn't for the life of him recall the colour of the robe he had been dressed in. He had been too young to know his colours anyway. His mother, father, and Jana gave him conflicting reports on what he had worn.

But he remembered how different his feet had appeared.

Where once his feet had been the colour of the soil beneath them, they had looked startlingly different. The colour of a sleepy sky before the sun could come and awaken it.

And that wasn't the only thing he remembered.

When the children had been dressed, the oldest priest had led them into the inner sanctum, right up to the Goddess in the hope that she may choose to infuse one of them with her being and bless the village.

To keep the children engaged as they waited, the priests led each child up to the deity, instructed them to touch her feet, and asked them to guess what she held in her fourth hand.

*No touching. Only looking.*

Their answers were varied and entertaining.

A ball.

A marble.

A grape.

A blueberry.

When it was Ari's turn, he had walked up to the Goddess and peered at her half-closed fist.

One of the children in the group chose that moment to begin whining, so the priest accompanying Ari momentarily left him to attend to the crying child.

Not knowing what to do, Ari looked up at the face of the deity. She seemed friendly enough, and so he said, "Show me what you have."

The deity opened her fist and showed him what no one had ever seen before.

A large blue drop of blood, emerging from a cut in her palm. Larger and larger it grew until, like a drop of water escaping a leaking faucet, it slipped away from her hand and fell into the copper pot that had been placed back on the floor beneath.

Just as quietly as she had opened her fist, she closed it again, so that only the bottom, bulging part of the teardrop was visible.

The priest reappeared at Ari's side, having settled the crying child, and asked, "So, what do you think the Goddess holds in her hand?"

"A blue teardrop," Ari said without hesitation. "She has a boo-boo on her hand. So she cries. Blue tears come out of that boo-boo."

The priest stiffened and hastily ushered Ari out of the inner sanctum. "You shouldn't tell such lies, especially not in such a sacred place. Gods don't get wounds. Never say such a thing again! The deity will punish you."

Ari didn't understand it then. But now, looking at his blue feet on the muddy brown floor of his hut, having recounted most of his adventures of the previous night to the village chief and to his parents, a realization dawned upon him.

The priest, who had taken it upon himself to care for the Goddess, had been terrified he'd be held responsible for any blemish on the deity. It hadn't been Ari's fault that he saw what he did.

And now, his parents and the village chief were terrified too. They would be blamed for what had happened to him, even though it wasn't really his fault or theirs that he had turned blue.

Perhaps, the bald leader of the tribe of the blue-skinned mystics was right.

The Great Spirit had indeed coursed through his veins last

evening just as surely as Hanadevi, the guardian deity of the land of Hanish, had responded to him years ago, when he had called out to her.

The village chief rose. "I will speak with our guests," he said. "In the meantime," he looked at Ari's father sternly, "take good care of your boy. He has helped save our village. Now it is our responsibility to save him."

# CHAPTER 9

# CONFESSIONS

"Do you remember the village festival when you were four years old?" Jana asked Ari as they walked through the woods behind their home.

Ari was under strict orders to not reveal his blue self to the world at large. At least, not intentionally.

Their father had wanted Ari to remain in the hut and not step out until they had heard back from the village chief, but their mother had reasoned with him.

*It could take the village chief days to tell us what to do next.*

*Ari's only a little boy. You can't lock up an eight-year-old in the house. He'll go mad and he'll drive everyone else mad.*

And when none of that seemed to dissuade their father from his decision to never let Ari step out of the house ever again, their mother had firmly threatened to report this utter wrongdoing to the village chief.

Their father had huffed out of the house at that.

"Where are you going?" their mother had asked his retreating back, but he had not paused to answer.

He had merely stomped out, leaving Ari, Jana, baby Nayo and their mother to decide their future course of action.

Eventually it was decided that Ari ought to carry on with his day as usual, except he was to try and stick to places where he was least likely to be seen.

Jana would accompany Ari, their mother instructed. Jana protested at first, and Ari knew why. If she had to remain by his side, she'd have to put away all plans to meet her lover.

But their mother reminded her that she and Ari had always been thick as thieves and that Ari needed now, more than ever, a friend by his side. That mollified Jana somewhat, and her chest even swelled up with pride.

Baby Nayo helped by staying calm throughout the discussion, which was conducted in an entirely civil and respectful fashion with their father and his temper out of the way, and finally provided his assent to all the decisions made by clapping his hands and butting mother on the chest. It was time to nurse.

"Funny you should bring up the village festival because that is what I was thinking about before the chief left," Ari said.

"You looked ugly that day."

"I'm sure father would have boxed your ears for saying something like that."

"I always thought all little children were beautiful," Jana continued as if Ari hadn't spoken. There was that faraway look in her eyes again. She had a large stick in her hand, and she swept it through the leaves on the forest floor in front of her as they walked. Left to right and back. But she wasn't paying much attention to what she was doing with the stick. "But then they painted you and all the other four-year-olds in that disgusting blue colour. You all looked very scary. As if you all had died and somehow come back from the dead."

Her voice caught on a choke, and Ari looked up to see tears run down her cheeks.

"I know what you mean," he said, slipping his hand into hers. She grasped him instantly, and the warmth of her hold made him feel brave once more. "I once saw baby Nayo turn blue," Ari said. "That day before I could come back with water from the next village. He was about to die?"

Jana nodded, and her tears fell to the ground.

"You know," Ari said, wiping a tear off her cheek, "Manaya said the Great Spirit once ran through you too."

Jana looked up, aghast, and Ari realized the prospect of an alien energy taking up residence in her body did not sound as appealing to her as it had to him. "Will I also turn blue?" she asked, horrified.

He shook his head and quickly said, "Not anymore! It doesn't run through you anymore."

"What do you mean?" Jana asked, still terrified at the slightest possibility that she may turn blue or sprout a horn or a tail or two.

Ari looked down at the forest floor and continued to walk. He couldn't look her in the eye as he said, softly, hoping she wouldn't hear him but would somehow understand him at the same time, "I saw you with that boy last night."

Jana gasped. She tugged at his hand, leaned forward to plant her face right under his eyes, and hissed, "You didn't tell anyone, did you? Did you?"

Ari was affronted. He and Jana had always kept each other's secrets, and he was miffed that she even thought he would ever rat on her. "I didn't," he hissed back, and pulled his hand out of Jana's. "You know I won't."

"Sorry, Ari," Jana pleaded and tried to hold his hand once more. Ari pulled himself away from her. "It's just … if father and mother ever found out, I'd be in a lot of trouble."

"I know," Ari mumbled. Tears slid down his cheeks now, and where they fell to the forest floor, sprung more teardrop plants.

He and Jana jumped back.

"Is this what's going to happen now every time you cry?" Jana giggled.

Ari found himself laughing too.

"Just don't make a tree erupt in the middle of our home," Jana continued, thrilled to be able to put a smile back on Ari's face.

"The next time father comes to hit me, that's exactly what I'll do."

Jana pulled him into a hug. "I wish he'd never come back home."

"I wish that too," Ari said.

# CHAPTER 10
# FOR THE GREATER GOOD

Whether it was the Great Spirit that throbbed in Ari's beating heart, or the remnants it had left behind in Jana's, or whether it was the doing of Hanadevi, the village deity, no one knew but the children's wish came true.

Their father did not come back home that evening.

At first, nothing seemed amiss. After their stroll through the woods in which they had not come across any other soul, Jana and Ari returned home.

Baby Nayo, who until then had refused to leave their mother's side, took an unexpected interest in Ari. He climbed on to Ari's lap, licked his hands, and rubbed his face.

"I'm not a toy," Ari pretend-squealed, which only made baby Nayo tumble into laughter and lunge towards his brother for another lick of his skin.

Jana helped with the household chores without being asked to, which caused mother to raise an eyebrow at Ari, who only shrugged in response.

The hut had an almost festive atmosphere that evening

without their father's anger threatening to ruin the joviality. Their mother cooked a sumptuous meal of flat bread and served a dish of vegetables—potatoes, carrots, peas—cooked in a spicy gravy.

After their meal, Ari and Jana dragged a cot outside the hut and lay there, dangling their limbs over the edges and watching the sky change colours. Crickets and other insects of the night sang a shrill farewell to the sun.

Their mother joined them, without baby Nayo by her side, just as the sun dipped beyond the horizon. She planted a lantern by the door to the hut, then squeezed herself between her two oldest children and hugged them to her sides.

There wasn't much to say, not at first. But when the fiery colours of the sunset sky gave way to the grave blue of twilight, Ari asked, "Will I remain blue forever?"

His mother squeezed his arm. "You may not remember this but when you were four years old—"

"I remember," said Ari at the same time that Jana said, "He remembers."

"What do you remember?" their mother asked, raising an eyebrow.

"You painted me blue," Ari said.

"That was the plan, yes." their mother nodded with a smile. "But you kicked up a right fuss about it. You didn't let us paint your face. You were the only child with blue limbs but a brown face. Like a world turned upside down. The colour of mud on the top. The sky at your feet."

"Really?"

Ari looked at Jana. Her brows were knitted in confusion. Her face was scrunched up in deep thought.

"But I remember he was blue," Jana said. "He looked quite scary. All the children looked terrifying."

Their mother looked at Jana with a mixture of concern and confusion. "But you weren't even there, sweetheart. How could you possibly have seen all that?"

Jana sat up straight. She pulled her braid and chewed on its ends. Their mother would have normally slapped her hand away but today she didn't try to stop Jana.

"What do you mean Jana wasn't there?" Ari asked. It was clear that Jana was not about to say anything. She had that faraway look in her eyes again, as if she was not here but somewhere else.

"She was unwell," their mother explained, not taking her eyes off Jana. "She had been unwell for several days. Her body was hot to the touch. So she stayed at home. Grandma stayed back with her."

"That was the night Grandma died," Jana whispered, tugging hard at the end of her braid.

"Yes," their mother said.

"I don't remember this," Ari said. "Why did Grandma die that night?"

"She died to save me. She took my sickness and made it hers," Jana blurted out.

"Jana!" their mother exclaimed. "That's not true. You mustn't say that. It wasn't your fault that Grandma died."

"It was," Jana cried. Big drops of tears streamed down her cheeks. Her shoulders heaved with every word she spoke. "She took my sickness, but she was too old. Her body was too frail. And it killed her. It should have killed me instead."

Their mother hushed Jana and pulled her to her chest. "Rubbish! Whoever put these ideas in your head!"

"But it's true," Jana cried. "She put her hand on my forehead and took a blue—"

A figure loomed over them. Ari and his mother looked up. The village chief stood at the gate. Jana pressed her face into her mother's shoulder. Her mother prised her away gently and stood up. Jana clung to her arm.

"Sir," she said, one arm still in her daughter's clasp and the other in her son's.

"Pardon my intrusion," the village chief said. "I came to have a word with your husband, Chandra."

Ari's mother hesitated. She looked at Jana, and then back at the village chief. It took her a few moments to reorient herself to this new demand placed on her. "The children's father hasn't returned home yet," she said, glancing at the night that had fallen around them.

"But it's already past dusk."

A strange sense of shame rose within Ari's mother, as if she ought to have been concerned about her missing husband instead of chatting away with her children outside their home. She hung her head and muttered, "You know how it is. He goes and comes of his own will. The baby keeps me busy." She craned her neck to look into the hut as if to reinforce baby Nayo's presence.

"How long has he been gone?" the village chief asked.

"He stormed out of the house shortly after your visit, Sir," she said.

"Did he say where he was headed?"

Ari's mother shook her head. She did not add that not only did her husband not confide in her but also she had not cared where he had gone. As far as she was concerned, she and the children had had a jovial day without their father.

"I have just returned from meeting the blue-skinned mystics," the village chief said.

Ari's mother looked up sharply and grasped her son a little tighter.

"They will not bother Ari anymore," the village chief continued. "In fact, they have agreed to leave the village tonight." He stepped towards Ari and squatted in front of him. "But you will do well to stay away from them, my lad."

"But they saved our village," Ari whispered.

"They have been of great service to us, yes, but their services are no longer required. Besides," the village chief said, "they are not our kind. They'd have probably felt out of place here sooner than later."

The village chief pulled himself up with some difficulty.

"But what about Ari's colour?" Ari's mother asked.

"The mystics said we must give it time. Ari's skin will transform back to its true hue," the village chief said.

Ari's mother pressed her hands together and bowed to the village chief. "Thank you, Sir," she said. "You've saved my child's life."

The village chief grunted, but not unkindly. "Now to find that husband of yours. If he shows up, send him to my place at once."

Ari's mother nodded, knowing well that her husband was likely to turn up drunk and completely incapable of making his way to the village chief's hut in the dark.

After the village chief left, their mother ushered Jana and Ari back inside the hut. Their soirée had been interrupted and would not resume, Ari understood without his mother having to spell it out for him. As if to confirm his suspicions, she brought the lantern back inside the hut and placed it close to the entrance, away from the cots.

"I must go and look for your father," she said once they were inside the hut. "You two stay here and look after baby Nayo. Jana, if Nayo wakes up, give him milk from the pot under his cot."

"But you can't go alone," Ari said.

His mother bent down and cupped Ari's face in her palms. "You mustn't worry about me, Ari. I won't be gone for long. I will head over to our nearest neighbours and ask them if they've seen your father."

"But I don't want him to come back," Ari sobbed. "It was so nice, just the three of us."

"Four," Jana hissed. She had already sidled up to baby Nayo and now lay, cuddling him. "And keep your voice down. Baby's asleep."

Which only made Ari sniff louder and harder. Ari's mother raked her fingers through his hair, then wiped his tears off his cheeks. "In the absence of your father, you are the man of the house now. Can you look after our home for one night? Your sister and your baby brother need you to be strong."

Ari nodded but he did not feel strong. He did not feel as if he had it in him to be strong if his mother were to leave.

His mother never went anywhere. She was the one who stayed at home. Except for those dreadful years of drought when she too had to accompany his father and every other able-bodied grown-up in Hanish to dig deeper into the step-well in search of water.

His memories of those years had already blurred, dissipated like threads of smoke coiling up towards the sky.

Hanish was a fertile land now. The paddy fields were lush.

Trees bearing mangoes and lychees had sprung up every-where. It was hard to picture what this place had looked like only a few months ago.

But much of the landscape was now also dotted with the new teardrop trees. A constant reminder of how close to extinction the village had come. A constant display of the role the blue-skinned mystics had played in saving the people of Hanish from certain death.

Their mother kissed Ari and Jana on the forehead, patted baby Nayo gently on his cheek, then lit another lantern and stepped out of the hut with a determined look on her face.

Ari plonked himself on his cot, from where he could see Jana holding on tight to baby Nayo. Her eyes were squeezed shut.

"Jana," he called out to her, but she did not stir. She wasn't asleep, he knew. She just didn't want to talk.

Ari put his arms behind his head and looked up at the ceil-ing. In the light of the lantern that flickered and threw wobbly shadows on the walls and the ceiling, he saw a small spider spin a web in a corner. Ari couldn't see the web at first, so fine was the spider's silk.

But he could tell from the way the spider seemed to walk on air, the way it paused in its methodical work and remained suspended there, about an inch away from either of the two walls or the ceiling that made up the corner it had chosen to build its home in, that the web was there. A hidden home for the spider to lie in wait for some silly insect to fall into its trap.

Ari jolted upright and sat on his cot, his heart pounding his chest so hard he couldn't breathe for an instant.

He glanced at Jana and baby Nayo. They were fast asleep.

He looked up towards the ceiling. The spider had shrunk into a corner. It had made itself so small, so invisible, Ari wouldn't have been able to see it if he hadn't known what he was looking for.

He piled two pillows on his cot, draped his blanket over them, then slipped out of the hut like a shadow, without a lantern to throw light on his path.

THE NIGHT WAS NOISY. At first, Ari assumed it was the susurration of leaves in the wind. He had chosen to take the shorter but darker route through the woods.

But he had not even gone ten paces when he felt a trickle of cold sweat down his back. He paused and looked up. The trees stood still. No wind to worry their heads.

The sounds seemed to drift from the village. Ari strained to hear, and at long last he realized it was the sound of people murmuring and shouting and talking all at once.

Ari broke into a run.

How could this be? He had only just left home.

Perhaps his mother had come back and found him gone. If his absence had been noted and people were already looking for him, he didn't have long to get to his destination.

It was only when he reached the step-well did it occur to him that the villagers may have been out looking not for him, but for his father. He burst out of the thicket of oaks that separated the step-well from the rest of the village.

The sight that greeted him was so unexpected it felt like a punch to his gut. It was as if a giant hand had emerged from the sky and swept through the area.

Gone were the caravans and the tents and the campfires. Gone were the children and their mothers. Gone was the congregation of hookah-smoking magic wielders.

There was no Manaya to behold. No bald leader of the tribe to talk about the Great Spirit and the magic his people wielded.

The ground was as it had always been — flat and empty — before the blue-skinned mystics had come and made it theirs, even if only temporarily.

Even the woods that had sprung to life behind the tents had been erased from existence. The horizon, a thin line separating the darkness of the sky from the more intense blackness of the land, appeared much more distant than Ari remembered.

Only the step-well remained. Full of water. Cradling a faux-moon and faux-stars on its chest.

Ari walked towards it. There was nowhere else to go.

In the pale light of the night, something black and inky crept along the edge of the step-well and disappeared into the water.

Without pausing to think, Ari squeezed his eyes shut and leapt into the well.

He waited for the splash. And then the sinking. But neither came. There was no breaching of the boundary between air and water.

He opened his eyes. As before, there were no eyes that needed to be opened. Only a willingness to surrender. Which he had exhibited the instant he had sprung up from the edge of the step-well, intending to plunge right into the water.

Here, too, it was noisy. The chattering of several creatures all at once.

He wondered if the villagers who had been out and about near the woods behind his home had already made their way here. Although why would they come here in the dead of the night? But the sounds were close. They came from all around him.

"Manaya?" he called out.

The chatter ceased momentarily, but picked up again, like foolish frogs resuming their midnight croaks after a brief hiatus in the moment when they lose one of theirs to a hungry serpent.

But the sounds were fast receding. Frogs hopping away from where the serpent had last struck.

"Manaya?" Ari called out frantically. He turned this way and that, his non-corporeal form easier to manoeuvre when he paid little attention to it.

There was only one thing on his mind. To find some answers.

But there was no response.

He made his way down, pierced through the side of the step-well, water becoming stone becoming mud of the earth. He finally emerged on the side just beneath where the blue-skinned mystics had stayed for a while, lived and laughed, cooked and feasted, lit fires and blew smoke out of their mouths.

The noise was louder here. A kind of susurration. Inhabitants of an entire kingdom whispering all at once.

The soil in the vicinity hummed and throbbed with unusual activity. It was soaked in a sickly-sweet scent.

The last time Ari had sojourned through the soil it had been alive. Worms wriggling here and there. Little critters digging and boring their ways through tiny tunnels.

But there was something extremely intense about the hum of activity around him tonight. Not the familiar drone of bees flitting from flower to flower in search of nectar. But the frantic and angry flutter of bees dislodged from their hive, solely focussed on protecting their queen.

A thousand wriggling maggots. Tiny white grubs, each no larger than a fat grain of cooked rice, squirming over one another. An entire planet of them digging through each other, reaching for something underneath the mass of them.

Ari dove into them for a closer look. There was something. Something that looked like a person asleep. Hands folded over the chest. Trousered legs down this end. Something oddly familiar about the fabric.

He came up the opposite way. And peered into his father's face.

His father?

This was his father!

His father was a corpse?

Ari sprang back. Maggot to soil. He shrank back from the corpse as fast as he could.

Thoughts collided in his consciousness. His father was dead. His corpse was buried under where the blue-skinned mystics had planted themselves for the past several weeks. What was father doing here? And why was he dead?

"He came to fight for you, you know?" Manaya's voice erupted through the soil like the unexpected boom of a gong.

A startled Ari spun around. But of course, like him, Manaya too was bodiless. Merely a voice. Merely a presence.

"Show yourself to me," Ari growled.

He wanted nothing more than to enter his body once again and put his limbs to good use. Punch Manaya in his face. Kick him to the dust. Tear his hair out. Bury him in the dirt where a thousand maggots would feast on his mortal remains.

"I am sorry, Ari," Manaya whispered.

Without his body, Ari could not feel the emotions he wanted to feel. Rage. Grief. Anger. He had come here for answers but was confronted with more questions instead.

"You did this," Ari hissed. "You and your tribe. Why? Tell me why," he screamed loud enough to make the earth tremble.

"Your father came here in the evening," Manaya said, his voice soft and soothing. "Shortly after the chief of your village left."

Ari made a quick calculation in his head. That must have been when he had indulged in a peaceful, joyful dinner with mother, Jana, and baby Nayo, feeling grateful that father was not around to ruin the occasion either with his drunkenness or his rage.

Something like guilt nudged his subconscious, but it was only a tiny spark. Likely a reaction born out of past conditioning. A reaction sprung from all the times he had been told what to feel and how to behave, lies told so often they had dripped into the very core of his being and crystallized like an immutable truth.

*Good children always respect their grown-ups.*

*You must do what the grown-ups say. They know better.*

Ari had not had any trouble following instructions doled out to him by his grandma or mother. But no matter how he twisted those words in his head, he could not justify the blows that his father had delivered him.

"He was drunk," Manaya said.

Ari snorted. No surprises there. But there was a hint of

pity in Manaya's tone that threatened to unmoor Ari. And he wanted nothing more than to crawl back into his own human skin and lie face-down on the ground and weep.

Weep for the father who no longer was.

Weep for the father he could have been.

Weep for the father he ought to have been.

"He wanted us to take away your blueness," Manaya said. "Said you'd become an outcast in the village if you remained blue."

Manaya paused, as if waiting for a remark from Ari. But Ari remained silent.

Manaya continued, "He was worried for you. He lunged at our leader, the one who spoke to you of the Great Spirit—"

"The one who pushed me into the water."

"The one who gave you a little nudge to help you overcome your fears and see for yourself what you are capable of, the magic that you wield, how the Great Spirit runs through you."

"So when my drunk father sprung at him, did your leader give him a little nudge too?"

"He merely sidestepped to save himself. Your father fell to the ground and hit his head, Ari. It was the fall that killed him."

Ari looked around wildly, but Manaya was nowhere to be seen. "And now you will tell me that the earth merely opened up and swallowed him whole. Your leader and your tribe had nothing to do with that, I suppose?"

"Don't you see?" Exasperation crept into Manaya's voice. "We couldn't leave him there, could we? Your people would have accused us of killing him as surely as you are doing right now."

"Is that why you are running away?" Ari said. With no eyes to shed tears from, all his grief spilled into his speech and choked his words.

"The chief of your village asked us to leave. Said your blueness was bound to raise many questions. Your people would have hurled accusations our way, even though we saved them. But after what happened to your father, it was clear that our time in Hanish had come to an end," Manaya confessed.

If Ari had had a head in that moment, it would have spun. How could the very people who saved an entire village have killed his father? They wielded magic that could resurrect the dead earth. Surely that was more than adequate magic to bring his own father back to life? He didn't know what to think.

"I don't believe you," he said. His voice was a raw whisper. "You saved an entire village, but you couldn't save one man?"

"We work for the greater good, Ari."

Ari couldn't believe his ears as Manaya continued, "Haven't you seen? You are the water, and you are the soil. You are the leaf of the teardrop tree, and you are also the maggots. You are your father and your mother, your sister and your brother, the chief of your village and his grand-daughter."

"Sheila? What does Sheila have to do with all this?"

"She was the first child of Hanish to die, wasn't she? It was her death that prompted the chief of your village to invite us here to your land."

The realization came as a shock to Ari. "Did your tribe kill her too?"

"No! No!" An unfamiliar panic lodged itself into Manaya's voice. "Ari! You mustn't think like that. We were miles away from Hanish when Sheila died, surely you remember that? But yes, there is always a price to be paid for magic. The Great Spirit demands a sacrifice. One life for the greater good. One life to save those of a thousand others."

Unable to contain the violent clash of all the emotions he needed to feel, Ari raced through the soil like an angry wind shrieking through the plains of a desert. So rapid were his movements that the earth trembled in his wake. The tremors he caused under the ground could be felt in the village, where his mother and their neighbours went door-to-door in search of father.

"You're lying," Ari screamed. "The Great Spirit took three lives. Not just one. Sheila. Father. And mine. There is no place for a blue-skinned boy in Hanish."

Manaya said nothing as Ari continued to thrash about, unable to stay in one place. The earth around them shivered.

The more Ari tried to outrun his thoughts, the faster and more intensely they came at him. Images of baby Nayo turning blue at the edges of his skin. Children painted in blue, the colour of Hanadevi's blood and tears. What Jana had said about the day of the festival, how grandma had taken the sickness out of her.

Ari paused so suddenly the quivering ground slammed back down into stillness. For an instant, even the maggots halted in their delirious feasting.

Something had changed irreversibly in the world around them. Like a rip through the fabric of the universe, a gash on its face from the east to the west, fracturing the ground beneath, piercing the air around, tearing through the skies above.

IN THE VILLAGE, the people fell to the ground as it stopped trembling under them. Losing their balance just as the earth seemed to have regained hers.

Ari's mother scrambled back to her hut, unwilling to be stopped by any force of nature, and gathered a teary-eyed Jana and a wailing baby Nayo in her arms.

"Where is Ari?" she screamed, the thought of yet another member of her household gone missing too excruciating to bear.

AND JUST AS SWIFTLY, the universe moved in to close whatever void had been created, stitch together wherever its skin had been split apart, and all its sentient beings once again moved and carried on with whatever had occupied them before this unwanted interruption.

For the thought that had stunned Ari into a momentary stillness now came out of his mouth, exploding like lava out of an angry volcano. Hissing at first. And then an explosion that drowned everything else.

"Grandma, too? Four lives?" Ari screamed.

His agony whooshed up from the earth and flew over the treetops like a fireball and drew the attention of the people of Hanish.

LYING on the ground that had first swayed under them and then knocked them off their feet, the villagers heard the anguished cry of one of their own.

With a unified roar, just as loud, in response, they roused their fallen selves to jump up and ran towards where the call had come from.

A call for help? A warning to stay away?

They didn't pause to think, but like a tidal wave slowly picking up momentum, they ran. They tripped and stumbled, their rage simmering and foaming, ready to unleash itself upon the target of their wrath and tear it asunder.

They made their way to the campsite of the blue-skinned people.

# CHAPTER II

# A FINAL DISAPPEARANCE

"It would have been Jana," Ari gasped. The words strangled his throat, so thick and impossibly true were they. But he spat them out, nonetheless.

For a truth was no truth until it was said out aloud. Not once. Not twice. But over and over again until no other version of it could possibly exist.

"It would have been Jana," Ari screamed again. It was the only act of violence he was capable of in this incorporeal form. His voice was the only weapon he had at his disposal.

"The Great Spirit works in mysterious ways, Ari," Manaya said. The plea in his tone was unmistakable. "It takes, yes. It demands a price, that is true. But it gives so much more. You see how it works in nature all around you. Individual sacrifices are made, yes, but always for the greater good."

"Stop saying that. The greater good. The greater good." If he could, Ari would have put his hands over his ears to stop those words from entering his subconscious. "Those words don't mean anything. It sounds like the kind of thing my mother or father would say if they didn't know the answer to something."

"Manaya!" A voice sounded around them. It was the bald leader of the tribe.

"I have to go, Ari," Manaya said. Something buzzed through the soil around Ari. Like an invisible worm burrowing the tiniest of holes to squirm through. "You must come with us." Manaya's voice was closer now. "You are one of us now. You belong with us. Hanish is no longer your home."

But how could Ari seek refuge with the very people who were responsible for his father's death? Even if they hadn't killed him, they had buried him and not said a word to anyone else. They had simply erased him from the face of the earth, just as they themselves had left, leaving behind no trace of their own existence.

"You are all hypocrites," Ari hissed, pleased with himself for recalling a word he had only come across in books but deeply saddened that he had finally found a good reason to use it. "Your leader has brainwashed you into believing all this is for the greater good. Maybe one day he will kill you too for the greater good of his tribe. What will you do then?"

"Manaya!" The voice boomed again around them. Closer. Menacingly closer. But its source was cleverly disguised by all the echoes it left in its wake.

Ari spun around, even though it was futile. He'd see no one who wished to remain concealed. But he knew he was being watched.

"Hanish is my home," he said as loudly as he could. "I will stay here."

"I am sorry, Ari." The whisper came like an out-breath, an exhale right next to him. It made him jump. It made him bolt.

Ari tore through the earth, away from his father's rotting corpse, broke through the stone wall of the step-well, zipped through the water, up, up, and up, broke the surface, then pulled himself over the edge and came back into his own body.

His hands gleamed indigo in the light of the moon, he saw with a quick glance, as he rolled away and away from the pool of water that emerged from the step-well after him, and now slithered like a venomous snake, a flat, shapeless one, moving so fast it was a mere flash in the night.

"Ari!"

"Ari!"

Countless voices called out. Not in unison.

There was no rhythm to it. Not like echoes. But several sporadic calls clashed together.

"Here!" Ari called out, his voice barely a whisper, as he ran towards the safety of the calls.

The pool of water that had been following him halted.

"Here, here!" Ari called out even louder.

The pool of water speedily crawled back towards the step-well, fell over its edges and disappeared into it.

Blotches of light bounced out of the woods. The villagers came, like water gushing forth from a broken dam, bearing flaming torches in their hands.

Ari scrambled up the nearest teardrop tree, wondering even as he did so why he was attempting to hide from the very people who were looking for him, who had come to ensure he was safe.

The answer came to him just as quickly as the question

had surfaced. He was still a blue-skinned boy. The mystics may have left, and he had chosen to stay behind, but he was a blue-skinned person nonetheless.

The mystics had assured the chief of the village that Ari's skin would once again become brown as earth.

But what if they had lied?

They had twisted the truth and lied about so many things there was no way to tell if they had spoken the truth about the colour of his skin or if it was yet another tale they had spun before making their getaway.

From his perch on the topmost branch of the tree, Ari saw the villagers rush past below him.

"The mystics are gone."

"What about Ari?"

"He must be here somewhere."

"What if they have taken him?"

"I heard him call out. 'Here, here,' he said."

"I heard that too. The call came from near the step-well."

"Keep looking!"

"Ari!" An anguished wail grabbed his attention. His mother came bounding out of the woods, baby Nayo on her hips, Jana at her heels.

Ari almost called out to them, but he stopped himself. And he knew why. They shouldn't be made to bear the burden of his curse. His blue skin had to remain his affliction alone.

The Great Spirit filling up his being had already attempted to claim baby Nayo and Jana. It had taken away his grandma. What if it came after his mother too? Now that his father was no more, who would look after baby Nayo and Jana if something were to happen to his mother?

No! Ari had to make sure the Great Spirit remained in him

and him alone. He had to make sure that his blueness, whether it was a blessing or a curse, would remain his alone. He would endanger no one by coming into their proximity.

The instant he resolved to stay away, his body trembled.

And then it crumbled.

Where once he had been perched on a branch, he now became the branch, the very essence of it, flowing from where it sprouted from the tree trunk, emerging into its own being, birthing many more branches in turn, as if it too were the trunk and the leaves and everything the tree was made of, not merely a single branch.

The essence of Ari flowed right through the branch and into a leaf at its very end, slid all the way to the tip of the leaf, then leapt into the air.

A wisp of blue.

Here now. Gone now.

Leaving no trace behind.

Like the blinking light of a glow-worm.

The twinkle of starlight.

The flash of a Blue Morpho.

Sun glinting off a piece of glass.

The light from a new moon.

Invisible to anyone looking for it.

# CHAPTER 12

# LOOK AT YOUR GODDESS AGAIN

It was Jana who brought baby Nayo to the temple this time. Baby Nayo. No longer a baby. But a young boy, all of four years old.

Ari almost gasped when he saw his little brother. For a child who had been kissed by death very early on, Nayo had grown into a healthy, little boy.

Nayo took his place in a row of children, all of the same age. Many were his friends.

Ari splashed about in the vat filled to the brim with the blue blood of the village deity, Hanadevi. When Jana soaked a sponge into the vat, the essence that was Ari clung to it and waited eagerly to be rubbed on Nayo's chest.

Nayo giggled as Jana began to paint him blue. Ari settled on Nayo's chest, right over his beating heart.

Laughter rumbled in Nayo's belly and came out of his mouth. Ari leapt onto it and drifted away.

This was as close to Nayo as he would get.

Like the breeze that would never feel the very cheeks it caressed. Like water that would never feel the very thirst it so easily quenched. Like the sun that could possibly not feel the very cold it aimed to dispel from the face of the earth.

Oh, well! It was worth a try, Ari sighed.

He darted through the air, pausing here and there for a closer look at the festivities from above. Nobody looked up at him.

Had anyone turned their faces upwards, especially the little children, they may have seen something.

A shimmer in the air. A dragonfly with sparkling wings, hovering for a moment, then bolting away. A brush stroke. Here now. Gone again.

But no one looked up. No one saw anything.

Even though it was the day Hanadevi was supposed to slip into the soul of a child and reveal the great mysteries of the universe to the villagers of Hanish.

"Why do you keep up with this farce year after year?" Ari asked the deity. He was now safely ensconced in her half-closed fist, the one that bled blue blood into a copper pot — the very pot that the earliest priests had first placed under Hanadevi's fourth hand and had dared not change ever since.

Ari had come to the temple that fateful night when he had resolved to not insert himself into the lives of his mother, Jana, and baby Nayo. And he had found he could remain in Hanish without actually being a part of the village and its people.

"It makes the people happy," Hanadevi said simply.

Occasionally, Ari had thought of sneaking into his old home to see how his mother, Jana, and baby Nayo were faring. But the deity forbade him from meddling in their destinies.

"This is what they are meant to live with, Ari, you will see,"

Hanadevi often cooed whenever Ari's grief transformed the drip of blue blood from her fist into a rapid trickle.

Ari and his father were still reported to be missing.

Endless searches near the step-well had yielded no clue, although by this time every person in the village was certain the blue-skinned mystics had either done away with the pair of them or fled the village with them in captivity. No one knew how close to the truth their conjectures were.

More than a year after the death of his father, Ari saw his family again. His mother, Jana, and baby Nayo, then a toddler, had come to pray to Hanadevi.

His mother was dressed in her best and finest. Her dress was stitched in the colours of autumn, which made her brown face glow.

Ari's heart sang at the sight of his mother. She would never have to wear a widow's garments. White robes, all colour leached away. A signal to the rest of the village to turn away from the piteous woman, cursed to outlive her husband. His mother would never be subject to such torment, for his father's death will remain unknown forever.

Jana, now taller than their mother, had also grown lovelier. There was a certain grace in the way she walked, slowly, unruffled, taking her time and space. There was something new in the way the villagers looked at her, as if assessing her suitability as a prospective bride for their own sons.

And baby Nayo was no longer a baby. Having discovered the use of his legs and feet to walk and run, he explored every corner of the temple with all his senses. Touching. Sniffing. Licking. Scratching. The priests were delighted at the spark of life the child brought with him.

The return of Ari's remaining family to the temple after

the tragedy that had befallen them had turned into a cause for celebration.

The Goddess was worshipped. Songs were sung. A feast was prepared. The entire village was invited. Delicacies were served. There was much singing and rejoicing, until Jana had yawned, and baby Nayo had fallen asleep on his mother's lap, and everyone decided it was time to go back home. There were still cows to be milked and land to be tended to the next morning.

That had been two years ago.

Ari's mother, Jana, and baby Nayo had not returned to the temple after that. They hadn't been devout temple-goers to begin with. Now with Ari and his father gone, his mother having taken to working on the land with the men of the village, everyone had accommodated their inability to be everywhere at all times.

But Jana had come now with four-year-old Nayo. Jana had grown more womanly since her last visit. She must have a lot of suitors, Ari thought, but Jana was unlikely to leave their mother alone until Nayo was old enough. That was Jana. Always dependable. The one you could count on.

Even now, she was stoic. There was a permanent smile on her face. If the blue-coloured four-year-olds appeared ghastly to her, she did not let it show on her face.

Ari did not have to wonder why their mother had chosen not to visit. The sight of all the blue-skinned four-year-olds in the temple yard would no doubt bring back memories of her own son, the one who had turned blue to save their village, the one who had disappeared shortly after.

"Come, children! Come, now!" The priest's voice rang out in the temple.

The four-year-olds bathed in Hanadevi's blue blood and draped in colourful robes that shone and sparkled like the Goddess's own golden garments lined up, giggling and jostling.

One at a time they were permitted into the inner sanctum. As instructed, each child first touched the stone feet of the deity and then proceeded to peer into her half-open fist.

Their answers were quite like the ones Ari's peers had given eight years ago when they had had the opportunity to sneak a peek into the Goddess's fist.

A ball.

A marble.

A grape.

A blueberry.

Some responses were ingenious too.

A blue eye.

A blue planet.

A blue moon.

As each child peered at the deity's fist, Ari peered out at them too. He looked into their eyes, took in their innocent faces, and whispered a blessing to each one of them.

And then came Nayo. He sat beneath the deity's fist and looked up. His thick black curls tumbled like storm clouds over his forehead and his ears.

His midnight black eyes took in not only the half-closed fist but everything else too. The spear in the deity's right hand. The everblooming lotus in her other right hand. The conch in her left hand. And the blob of blue in her other left hand.

"What do you see, Nayo?" The priest attempted to inject

curiosity in his question, but Ari discerned the impatience it held.

So many children still queued up outside, waiting for their turn. How would this event conclude on time if Nayo lingered, inspecting the entire inner sanctum as if he was about to take up residence here?

Nayo looked up and into the deity's eyes, quite like Ari had done, as if he was about to pose her a question.

And then he changed his mind and looked back at her fist. He squinted at it for a few moments.

Then his face broke into a smile, and he said only one word, "Ari?!"

~ THE END ~

*Eager for more fantasy fiction involving gods and humans? Dive into the adventures of Infinity, a Harbinger of Death, in Dying Wishes, a contemporary fantasy novel set in Canada and weaving Hindu mythology and South Indian folklore into a quest for belonging across different worlds.*

# ENJOYED BLUE-SKINNED MYSTICS?

Thank you for reading *Blue-Skinned Mystics*!

If you loved the book, I hope you will consider writing a short review—even a simple line or two—on the site where you bought the book or on any review site such as Goodreads.

Publishing is still driven by word of mouth, and when you leave a review it helps other readers decide this is a book worth reading. Thank you for your help in spreading the word.

You can also sign up to my monthly newsletter on the joys of writing and reading to stay updated on new releases as well as receive additional works of fiction available exclusively to subscribers and, most importantly, to stay connected!

https://thedreampedlar.com/newsletter

# AUTHOR'S NOTE

Dear Reader,

I have attempted to write this note to you on three different occasions now, separated by months.

This is mainly a result of me believing each time that the book wasn't quite ready for publication. At first, it was the book cover that was nagging me. Then it was the proof-reading that was taking time and caused this tale to languish some more.

Now that I have finally finished giving this book a long last look before it goes out into the world, I can't help but feel a little stunned.

I had finished writing this story back in January 2022. More than three years ago! I remember very little of what had inspired me to write this tale, but I also seem to have forgotten much of the story itself, barring the first chapter, which I had read over and over again in my attempts to bring this manuscript to a publication-ready format.

This time, I read this tale as a reader would. As someone completely unfamiliar with the story would.

I felt a great sense of pride at the choices our eight-year-old hero, Ari, made throughout this story.

Delving into the theme of 'the greater good' has also brought to mind the classic 'trolley problem'. You're very likely already familiar with it.

You're navigating a trolley (or a train) that is hurtling down a track on which five people are standing. They will certainly get killed if you keep going.

You have the option of pulling a lever and diverting the trolley/train to another track, where only one person is standing.

Would you do so and let one person die? Or would you let the trolley/train continue on its original path and let the five people die?

I recently watched a Tamil movie, *Viduthalai*. The word means *liberation*.

In two parts, the story is told from the point of view of a newly recruited police constable who is part of an investigation aimed at capturing the leader of a separatist group.

The trolley problem is posed in that movie too with an additional twist.

The captured leader of the separatist group notes that most people respond to the trolley problem by claiming that they'd rather save five lives at the expense of one.

"But what if that one person is your mother? Or your child? Someone you know and love?" the character asks. "Would you still make the same choice?"

This is a question worth pondering, especially in these times when it appears that the powers-that-be — heads of organizations, institutions, even nations — are tasked with making tough calls and decisions that do not affect them or their loved ones directly.

It seems callous that the fates of countless nameless, faceless people depend on the whims and fancies of those who are least affected by the outcomes of their decisions.

It reminds me of that scene in Oppenheimer when U.S. officials are deciding which cities to decimate in Japan with the atomic bomb, and Kyoto was struck off the list because one of the decision-makers had been there for his honeymoon.

I understand the movie is a dramatized version and doesn't portray the entire truth, but the scene certainly points to the arbitrariness and subjectivity that can steer decisions with enormous consequences.

We're all human. We're all flawed. And I believe we're all doing the best we can; even when we make the most selfish of decisions, it's quite literally the best we're capable of in that moment of time.

Besides, these are the thoughts that I'm left with *after* having the read the story from start to finish one last time before publication. I doubt these were the sentiments that propelled me to write the story in the first place!

Those reasons and memories are lost to time now. But I vividly remember the joy of writing this tale; the delight of penning down certain scenes came back in a rush as I read them while preparing the manuscript for publication.

I certainly hope you too felt a certain stirring of your soul as you read this story.

Thank you for reading this far. I'd love to stay in touch with you. And I hope you'd like to stay connected with me too.

If you'd like to accompany me further on my author journey, sign up for my monthly newsletter. *Monthly Missives from The Dream Pedlar* goes out on the last Sunday of every month. Subscription is free.

You will be the first to hear of my forthcoming works. I also include updates on my writing life, book recommendations, free short fiction, and occasional surprises.

Thank you for staying with me this far. Climb aboard at https://thedreampedlar.com/newsletter!

*~ Anitha Krishnan*
*Burlington, Ontario*
*Thursday, 18 September 2025*

# MORE BOOKS BY ANITHA KRISHNAN

https://thedreampedlar.com/books/

## NOVELS & NOVELLAS

### *Dying Wishes*

*Finalist, 2023 Rakuten Kobo Emerging Writer Prize in Speculative Fiction*

An expansive contemporary fantasy novel weaving Hindu mythology and South Indian folklore into a quest for belonging across different worlds — the World of Mortals and the World of Gods, India and Canada, the past and the present, the world outside and the one within.

### *Erased from Existence*

An intriguing paranormal mystery in which a fifteen-year-old is erased from the memories and perception of everyone. Trapped in oblivion, she will have to unearth and reveal long-buried family secrets to escape.

### *The Land of No Reflection*

A feisty fantasy tale of two sightless young women on the run from their homeland, having committed the unpardonable crime of seeing.

### *In Search of Leo*

A heart-stirring fantasy tale exploring the gamut of emotions that loss and grief can stir.

SHORT STORIES

### *A Benevolent Goddess*

An endearing story of a goddess who is punished for her desire to
help human beings but is unable to find salvation by any other
means.

### *The Mind Meddler*

A thought-provoking short fantasy story on the games The Mind
Meddler plays by sneaking thoughts into people's minds, until he
meets the one person who can resist his unkind mischief.

### *Mrs. D'Souza's Dispute With God*

A touching fantasy short story in which a school teacher, Mrs.
D'Souza, dies unexpectedly and sets out in search of God to demand
answers to her burning questions on life and death.

### *Your Mother's Nightmares*

A bold collection of troubling, twisted tales scoured from the
terrifying emotional depths of the motherhood experience.

### *Tales For Dreamers: Volume 1*

A whimsical collection of 100 flash fiction tales where the mundane
morphs into the magical, the everyday shape-shifts into the
exceptional, and the inconceivable becomes the inevitable.

POETRY

### *Hello, Dreamer! Poems & Dreams*

An eclectic collection of 100 short poems encompassing musings on the universe and its mysteries, nature and human life, my secret longings and fears, love and heartbreak, the sun and the moon, the stars and the seas, light and shadow, and joy and nostalgia.

# ABOUT THE AUTHOR

Anitha Krishnan is a speculative fiction author and an award-winning poet. Her fantasy novel, *Dying Wishes*, was a finalist for the 2023 Rakuten Kobo Emerging Writer Prize in the Speculative Fiction category.

She has lived in and left pieces of her heart in many places across the world including Singapore, Australia, Canada, and most of all in her beloved birthplace, India. She presently lives in Burlington, Ontario with her husband and their cherished child.

Sign up to her monthly newsletter at
https://thedreampedlar.com/newsletter
to stay connected and to receive heartfelt musings, exclusive updates, book recommendations, free fiction, and more!

www.ingramcontent.com/pod-product-compliance
Lightning Source LLC
Chambersburg PA
CBHW031547310726
48971CB00008B/2655